Honoria

by erAto

Alumbra Publishing

2019

Honoria
part of the *Regency Romantics*,
© 2017 Talia Felix

Reprinted by
Alumbra Publishing
2019

978-1-7341846-3-1

Year:

1805

CHAPTER 1

She had done everything that she was supposed to do. She had scrubbed her teeth daily with a small brush, and followed the most up-to-date dental advice, but still the toothache came. It had begun its life as a mere discomfort when exposed to hot or cold, but over the months has grown increasingly sensitive and increasingly painful. Now, it had reached a point where the anguish was constant and undeniable. God had not seen fit to save her from this. After three days at full vigor, the torturous pain of the tooth was too unbearable to endure any longer. As it said in the Bible, "if thy right eye offend thee, pluck it out, and cast it from thee: for it is profitable for thee that one of thy members should perish, and not that thy whole body should be cast into hell." To alleviate the pain, it was going to require casting out a tooth.

18 year old Honoria did not like the idea of losing one of her teeth — especially since the

tooth-pulling process was sure to be violent and painful itself — but Honoria's guardian, Rev. Mr. Burney, set up his gig and took his poor suffering ward to the nearest market town, about 90 minutes away from their home in the village of Blore. She feverishly waited for the dreaded event, resolved to bear the unspeakable operation provided it would only ease her sufferings. There were wealthy dentists who could perform elaborate procedures — tooth transplants, denture-making, fitting braces, filling cavities — but it was not to one of these that Honoria was headed. She was to patronize a common tooth-extractor.

When they arrived in front of the tradesman's house, made recognizable by an immense wooden signboard where the name of "Coghill" sprawled in enormous pumpkin-colored letters, Honoria gasped for breath. Her young face was beaded with perspiration. A horrible fear shook her, a trembling crept under her skin; then suddenly a calm ensued, the suffering ceased, the tooth stopped paining.

"Perhaps this is too severe a remedy," she said. "Perhaps I can bear the tooth a while longer."

"This is your first toothache; and I can promise you, it will not improve any with time," replied Mr. Burney, who himself was obviously fewer some teeth he had possessed at birth, and knew the ways of the toothache.

She remained, stupefied, on the roadside; Mr. Burney had to urge her along. Finally, she stiffened against the tooth-borne anguish, mounted the dim stairway, running up two steps at a time to the fourth story. She found herself in front of a door where an enamel plate repeated the name of Coghill, now in blue letters. Mr. Burney knocked upon the door, and Honoria, terrified by the great bloody spittles which she noticed coating the steps, resolved to endure his toothache all her life and asked Mr. Burney if they might turn back.

At that moment an excruciating cry pierced the partitions, filled the cage of the doorway and glued Honoria and her guardian to the spot with horror, at the same time that a door was opened and an old servant woman invited them to enter.

Honoria's feeling of reluctance quickly intensified into that of terror. Speechless, she was ushered into a drawing room. Another door creaked and in entered a terrible grenadier dressed in a frock-coat and black trousers. Honoria and her guardian followed him to the chamber.

From this instant, the young girl's sensations were confused. She vaguely remembered having sunk into a chair opposite a window, putting a finger to her tooth — which action stirred the pain all the worse — and moaning: "It is this one which has been paining me."

The man immediately suppressed these explanations by introducing an enormous index finger into her mouth. Muttering, he took an instrument of iron from the table. Then the game began. Clinging to the arms of her seat, Honoria felt a cold sensation in her cheek, and then began to suffer unheard agonies. She beheld stars. She stamped her feet frantically and bleated like a sheep about to be slaughtered. Her guardian, overseeing, tried to offer soothing words.

"It will not take long, it will be over soon," he assured her, wincing with sympathy pains.

A snapping sound was heard: the molar had broken whilst being extracted. It seemed that her head was being shattered, that her skull was being smashed; she lost her senses, howled as loudly as she could, furiously defending herself from the man who rushed her afresh as if he wished to implant his whole arm in the depths of her bowels, brusquely recoiled a step and, lifting out the tooth attached to the jaw, brutally let her fall back into the chair. Breathing heavily, his form filling the window, he brandished at one end of his forceps, a discolored tooth with blood at the base.

Faint and fallen, Honoria spat blood into a basin. Tears were running down her face and her lips were smudged with crimson liquid. The old woman who had guided them into the room took the tooth and wrapped it in a piece of newspaper for Honoria to take home with her, as a souvenir of the experience.

"I have some unhappy news for you," said the tooth-puller, once Honoria seemed to regain sentience. "On the other side is another tooth which is decaying, too. If you wish, it can be left as it is; but in a few months you will have these same pains again. I recommend that it be taken out, while you are still here."

Wincing, Mr. Burney nodded his own approval of the plan, but had to confirm it to Honoria. "Can you endure one more? It is for the best to have it all done at one time..."

Knowing that her guardian was correct, Honoria shut her eyes and agreed. The whole procedure was repeated once more, Honoria's pain being made no less severe for the foreknowledge of what was to come. She could hear the tooth being drawn up by its roots, like pulling a stubborn vegetable from the ground, amidst the blinding agony she experienced. Soon it was out, and one more bloody piece of her body was wrapped in paper and presented. Honoria was not able to stand by herself and needed to be helped up by Mr. Burney, who paid the technician his fee.

Expectorating blood, in her turn, down the reddened steps, she was guided back to the gig. Mr. Burney asked if she might be interested in eating or shopping whilst in town. Honoria refused, and begged only to be taken home immediately.

Back in her own room at their little house in Blore, Honoria crawled into bed and did her best to sleep away the pain. Her governess, Miss Hooper, checked in on her from time to time.

Honoria Wright was the natural daughter of someone important. That he was a Marquess was all the Honoria herself knew of him; she had never met him nor, to her knowledge, been regarded in any way by this man. Her unfortunate mother, Deborah Wright, had died while Honoria was still too young to preserve any memory of what went on around her, and it was Rev. Mr. Burney who had agreed to take on poor little Honoria as his charge. Mr. Burney was aware of the true parentage of young Miss Wright, but so far had withheld from her the actual identity of her father, feeling it would do little good for a secret daughter to know such information. Thus she had been raised by Burney in the rural village of Blore, where he had charge of the church. He had raised her, father-like, and with as much indulgence as his income would allow. Nevertheless, her actual father *did* know of her and of her location, and did from time to time send to Mr. Burney some money for her upkeep. This money, which Mr. Burney had never depended upon nor expected, was merely set aside on Honoria's behalf. Burney thought it might one day serve as a dowry for her. Being that she was of noble blood, he hoped that one day she might be able to marry back into such a suitable state; it was a condition her bloodline expected of her. He dreaded especially any possibility that she could instead take after her mother and wind up *not married at all*. A handsome dowry would assist her in achieving the happy outcome he so wanted her to achieve.

The recent adventure of the pulled teeth had set him to thinking about this matter more intently. Honoria was old enough that her teeth were beginning to fail; this certainly meant that she was old enough to consider a marriage. Beauty and youth were some of the best draws to a husband, and the dental decay was a sign that both would one day fade.

It was a fact, Mr. Burney came to realize, that Honoria would have to be sent out of the village in order to locate for herself a husband worthy of her status. The old clergyman began without delay to write to whatever friends he could think might be willing to take on Honoria; particularly those who resided in some sensible place like London or York or Edinburgh where the marriage market could offer her some finer prospects.

It was at last that some relatives of the late Mrs. Wright, the Everdeens, who knew Honoria a little, responded favorably to Mr. Burney with an offer to host Honoria at their residence in the city of Bath, which at the time was one of England's largest cities and was considered a fashionable place for the wealthy to pass their time away from London. In those charming old days London was a place of solid filth, with famously unbreathable air; but Bath was a clean, fresh city, with good water and many entertainments. It was an excellent opportunity for Honoria, even if there was some risk that she would be exposed to immoral influences amidst the gaiety of that town. Mr. Burney had raised Honoria strictly according to church principals, and she had been always obedient: she did not overindulge in life's pleasures and she disdained all vice. Yet, Burney worried — away from his care, might she fall under the spell of bad influence? Immorality was as much in her lineage as was nobility — would she slide to the wrong end of her nature? Yet it was necessary that it be proved. There was no other way for Honoria to reach her potential, good or bad, unless she was left to the ways of the world.

By this time, the passage of a couple months left Honoria recovered from her dental extractions, though she now, when taking meals, had to eat much more slowly and awkwardly. As she speedlessly chewed her dinner, Mr. Burney delivered to her the good news that some of her cousins in Bath wished to have her come for a visit with them in July.

Honoria, who had never gone any farther from Blore than some of the nearby market towns, was simultaneously annoyed and delighted by the prospect before her. She was silent for a long time, not certain of what she could say in response. The concept of going so far from her familiar home to dwell with near-strangers in a strange place about which she knew nothing, seemed far from pleasing to her; and yet, she was young and a youthful energy and curiosity did urge her to consider its potential. Maybe it would be fun? Maybe the place would be exciting and beautiful? And her cousins always had seemed like nice people, when they had visited her in Blore.

"I should like to have time to think it over," said Honoria. "But what is the reason for this sudden invitation? Is it known to you?"

The good old Reverend was forced to admit that he had sought to gain such an offer for her. "You have lived so long in this village, and while I do hope that your simple and honest country life will not be forgotten, we must begin to look to your future. You are at an age where Nature has provided you with its peak of beauty, vigor and health. Is it right to keep you hidden and shut away at such a time — a brief time, that will fade before you know it? I do not wish to rush you into hasty action that might, far from my wishes, bring you to a future you regret; but the short time of your youth will pass whether you take action or not, and it is advised you be introduced into the world during this point. You should think of your life in 10 years — where would you be? Will you live here, in this tiny village, with an old man such as a myself (if I am even living by then?) Or would you be settled with a family of your own, existing as a respected and beloved wife to some fortunate gentleman?"

Honoria's cheeks pinkened as she considered the possibility, which undeniably did appeal to her. To be married, to be happy as a wife and mother! To be mistress of her own house, instead of subject in another's! This was a future she did fondly wish for, although her happy life in the country and the natural desire not to change from a good situation, had always keep dormant these wishes. But now Mr. Burney was firing her breast with a fresh yearning for these things. A happy future could soon await if she would only bear the small risk of trying for it. By the end of dinner she had agreed to his idea of going to visit with her cousins, the Everdeen family, in Bath. There, she might be able to locate, for herself, a man to whom she could be gladly bound for life.

CHAPTER 2

Before she left by the mail-coach from Ashbourne, Mr. Burney personally handed Honoria a £10 note and told her to simply write to him if she should find herself in need of anything more during her trip. There were people in England who did not earn £10 in an entire year — for it to last a young girl on a 10-week trip to Bath should not be out of the question; yet knowing the reality of fashion, city life, and so forth, Mr. Burney was prepared for anything. He had the secret stash of money ready and waiting; though Honoria's hosts, the Everdeens, would naturally be expected to cover the bulk of her expenses. Her housing, meals and other necessities would be part of their hosting duties, but it was possible she was going to require some expensive new outfits, hairdressing and so forth in order to fit in with the Bath society, and draw herself the man of her dreams.

It was a long trip by the mail-coach and Honoria was a little frightened to be alone and surrounded only by strangers, for so long a time, in such isolated locations. But the mail-guard, armed with his guns, keeping watch over the letters and packages being sent, offered her some sense of security. In the fast coach it was about a full day and night's travel, and when the vehicle stopped in front of the White Hart in the center of Bath, Honoria already felt exhausted and ready to go home.

The outside of the inn was a mess of coaches — mail coaches leaving and taking letters for every part of the country, traveler's coaches depositing those who wished to stay at the famous inn, and those of the city travelers just passing through the narrow street. Yet the city itself was beautiful — Greek style buildings cut from a smooth and slightly yellow-hued stone, which looked all the prettier in the sunlight. There was little of nature in the surroundings, but that was to the taste of the day; trees and plants were regarded as ugly obstructions to the beauty of mankind's fine architecture. Honoria was now here with the challenge of doing likewise — foregoing nature to become worthy and sophisticated. She was to become a citizen of the world!

Honoria stepped down from the coach with her baggage in hand, and though she meant only to locate the front entrance of the building, she became confused in the collection of vehicles, and found herself making a circle the entire ways around the building, yet still not finding anything that seemed a reasonable front door. Thus she went around the building to the back entrance, which had appeared like the only real way inside. It was a servant's entrance, but Honoria assumed it must be the real way in, since the crowds gave an appearance that no other point was possible to enter. The staff members who saw her come in gave her some questioning looks, and assumed from her appearance and the baggage in her hand that she was either a visitor or was associated with one. A footman at last approached her and asked where she was going; she replied that she was awaiting someone in the front room, and he showed her there promptly.

When Honoria entered, she could immediately see the Everdeen family waiting for her, staring out the windows in expectation of seeing Honoria entering at any moment. It had been a few years since they had seen one another but she could still recognize "Aunt" Elizabeth (who was in actuality her cousin, but a significant age difference made Elizabeth a *de facto* aunt.) Also she knew "Uncle" Edward, the spouse of Elizabeth, and Elizabeth's daughter Margaret, who was only three years younger than Honoria and was more like what one imagined of a cousin for her.

When Honoria entered from behind them, she was obliged to call out to get their attention.

"Elizabeth? Edward?"

They turned to face her, surprised that she had come inside without being observed.

"Oh! Honoria, we did not see you!" said Elizabeth.

Margaret, being 14 years old and at that age where everything said comes out as an insult, accusingly said to Honoria, "Did you just come out from the *kitchen*? Ugh."

Honoria shrank a bit, realizing too late that such an action might have come off as unseemly. "Oh, I *am* sorry. I could not find any other entrance to the building."

"Did you try the front door?" said Margaret, in that same destructive tone.

Elizabeth stepped in kindly, in order to provide Honoria with a friendlier welcome. "Well, whatever means it took, you are now here. And we are so happy to see you! Come and give us a hug," she said, rising to embrace her young cousin.

The women embraced, and now it was Edward's turn to speak to the new arrival. "Are you hungry?" he asked. "We can take some refreshment here at the inn before heading back to the house — it is renowned for its excellent food."

Honoria agreed that she was in fact very hungry after the long journey, and some food was ordered.

Elizabeth was embarrassed by her daughter's bad behavior, but she hoped that Honoria's good influence might effect her. In fact, the hopes of improving her daughter were the motive behind her invitation to Honoria — Elizabeth was an enthusiastic but unsuccessful mother, having one surviving child out of six, and that one rather spoiled and temperamental. Honoria's visit was something she looked forward to as an educational experience, and an opportunity to try her own skills on a new artform. Elizabeth understood that the real reason for her young cousin's visit was to prepare her for the marriage market. Having little to occupy herself in general, and knowing the importance that a good or bad marriage would hold over her poor little cousin's life, she agreed to take upon herself the activity of matchmaker and finisher. She was glad for the chance to do something useful, and for the opportunity to learn in advance how she might prepare for her own daughter's eventual coming-out. Now she had to determine how well advanced Honoria really was in the game of courtship. She could see at once that Honoria's clothing was several years out of date, still wearing the fluffy, gathered skirts of circa 1800, and that she seemed to take little care about her hair since in the country there were not many great hairdressers. And of course she had just demonstrated that sort of simple country practicality where getting into the building at all was viewed as more important than doing it with dignity. *That* would have to be worked on, too.

"Honoria," said Elizabeth, "I remember that the last time I saw you, you were receiving your lessons in dancing. How did that ever turn out?"

"I think I have learned them well," said Honoria. "I have been to some Assemblies at Ashbourne and Derby, and as of yet there has been no dance I did not know."

Elizabeth went on with some like interrogations and was able to determine that Honoria already knew all the basics for a woman her age. The job, in that case, was going to be little more than showing her the culture and refinement needed to polish her up. So far, Honoria seemed like she was a pleasant enough girl: honest, sweet-natured. It should be a simple enough task to render her attractive.

After a quick meal, the family went to their home — a townhouse located on Broad Street. It wasn't one of the most fashionable places in town, but they did have a Viscount living next door. As they pulled up, Elizabeth warned Honoria, with a little embarrassment, that women often came to call upon the neighbor

Viscount — a deed that was not normally smiled upon — but that in deference to his status and because it was not for anyone to judge, this activity was always overlooked.

Honoria was a bit horrified by the thought of dwelling beside such a person, and horror even turned into a tinge of outrage when considering that such a person held such an honorable position as a Viscount. When she expressed concern about her safety while being housed next to such a man, both Elizabeth and Edward let out a laugh.

"I promise you," said Elizabeth, reassuringly. "You are very safe. He only has very *particular* women over; and the kind of women he has over, are not the kind of women you are likely to become acquainted with." She also reminded Honoria that even if she ever were to recognize one of the Viscount's women-friends, to only ignore them and act with any necessary courtesy towards them; "There is no reason to humiliate them, afterall; for we do not really know what goes on. Gossip is very much frowned upon in Bath, moreso than in other cities."

Indeed, in the mind of Honoria, that she had no right to judge was fast remembered — afterall, her own parents had probably been in a situation very similar to what went on next door, based on what information she knew of them. She instantly felt ashamed, and let her mind wander from these reflections.

Honoria was shown to a makeshift bedroom, converted from what was normally used by the Everdeens as a library. An old but suitable bed had been brought in for her, and a table was cleared off for her to utilize as a vanity. She had even been supplied with a new novelty chamber pot, which contained a ceramic image of Napoleon built into the bowl.

The evening was spent largely in getting Honoria settled into the house and ensuring she was familiar with the layout of the place, knew the servants, and such basics. Honoria was glad when bedtime finally came around, though once she was settled in her sheets she found that sleep was not easy to come in the strange new space.

The next several days of acclimation found Honoria growing more at ease with her situation. Activities were frequently devised for the girls to keep them busy; a shopping trip here, a visit to the print-makers there. After about a week, Elizabeth maneuvered Honoria over to the dress-maker's, where she wanted her to purchase some new clothing.

"...And when the gowns are ready, we can take you to an Assembly. But you should have something new to wear; those outfits, that are so usual in the county, are not very familiar here in the city, where fashions can change so rapidly."

Honoria looked through the dressmaker's selection of fashion books, observing the more lean-cut silhouettes; and she at last picked out what Elizabeth feared to tell her was the ugliest dress-pattern of all; but it was a legitimate piece of fashion, so Elizabeth did not speak and allowed Honoria to get whatever it was she wanted. The dressmaker predicted she could have the outfit ready in about two weeks.

Honoria also picked out two other outfits, for walking and for daytime. She had at least one good set of clothes on the way, now; and that evening, Elizabeth and Margaret set about helping Honoria to alter the clothing she already possessed, so that it would better fit the new fashions.

"If we remove the skirt, lift the waist, and cut out some of the bulk before reattaching," said Elizabeth as she examined what Honoria regarded to be her best dress, "it should look tolerably to the mode." It was a simple white muslin frock, of the sort that had been beloved a few years before. Mr. Burney did not often remember to keep Honoria up to date on fashions, and living in the country meant that the news of the modes was not always well known or circulated in the region.

The work of the three women allowed Honoria to have a respectable outfit by the next day, and her wardrobe improved throughout the week, though Honoria was annoyed that the hem of her skirts were now a consistent two-inches higher than she would have wished; this was the result of raising the waists. She began to sew ruching and flounces onto the skirt of anything that could bear it, in an effort to reveal a bit less ankle, despite Elizabeth and Margaret's protests that a bit of ankle was not unacceptable.

When Honoria tried on one of her improved gowns for the first time, she was surprised to observe that the narrower skirt was affecting how she walked — her stride was wider than the new allotment of cloth, and each time she took a step, she could feel the fabric catching her at the ankles, nearly causing her to stumble as her movement was interrupted.

When the ladies set out together to take a walk to the Crescent to pass the time, Honoria made it about one block from the house before she misstepped and fell to the ground. Elizabeth and Margaret helped her up, and the embarrassed

Honoria assured them she was alright; but by the time they reached the Crescent the seam of the skirt had a large tear in it, and a string of ruching trailing off and behind. Of all the things Honoria should have to be taught, nobody had imagined that among them should have been how to walk!

CHAPTER 3

Honoria sat at the window of her library-bedroom and watched the local activity as another woman was leaving the house of the mysterious Viscount next door. The Viscount himself, she had not chanced to observe; but she imagined him as an old man, bent with age, with a general sense of menace about him, and upon his withered and age-spotted face wearing ever a look full of greed and heartless lust. In a word: Nosferatu.

Having been brought up under the care of the Reverend, her brain had been filled with a very binary view of the world as a place of clear rights and wrongs; works of God and works of the Devil; yet Bath seemed to be a strange and backward place where wrongs were accepted and rights were frowned upon... except when they weren't.

One complexity that was often at the back of her mind, was her parents. She knew vaguely of their story — her mother was of a good family but had met and had a child with a Marquis, who for whatever reason did not marry her, and after that time, he had little more involvement with either the child he produced or the ruined woman he left behind. Poor Deborah, mother to Honoria, had been able to live off the charity of the church for the few years of life she had been left to enjoy, but she had been disowned by her family. After Deborah's death, a few relatives had come forward with interest in Honoria, not wishing to see an innocent child punished for the misdeeds of her parents; but Mr. Burney had already promised Deborah that he would personally care for the daughter, and he knew that Deborah herself mistrusted the motives of a family who would disown her, fearing they would either seek to turn her daughter against her memory, or that they might try to use Honoria as some kind of pawn to extort money from the Marquess (whose identity was known to a few select family members.) So he stood by his word and raised Honoria, allowing her to receive only visits from family members; which is how the Everdeens had come to know her. With Elizabeth being so much older than her cousin (an age difference of 18 years) they had not had a relationship as close friends, but Elizabeth had been married about the same time that Honoria was born, and free from any family proscriptions against visiting her little cousin, she had taken a fondness for the little girl and had spent time with her in the dull little village of Blore as often as time had allowed, which was, admittedly, pretty rare.

In observing the antics of the disquieting next door neighbor, Honoria seemed to be often reminded of her father, a man of whom she had rarely thought since she knew practically nothing about him. It was not even entirely clear to her whether her father knew that she existed. Troubled by these thoughts, she wished that Mr. Burney were at hand for her to ask him such questions. But the distance between them being as it was, the only comfort she could get was from writing to him; and so she wrote an inquiry about the identity of her father, or what was known about the man.

It took a few days for the letter to reach Burney, and a few more for his reply to reach Honoria, but a reply was received. Burney had not hesitated, and in reply to his ward, he wrote the following:

My dear Honoria:

The discoveries of the world, in Bath, as to the nature of morality and immorality, of virtue and vice, and even of good and evil, are discoveries which I have known you must make; yet my heart does quake at the thought of it, and it is my utmost hope that you shall not take this observation of blurred lines to suggest that the world grants you any permission to fall into vice, yourself. I urge you to conduct yourself as always, with modesty and integrity and virtue, and let these observations remain to stand as nothing more than observations. The Honoria I have always known is a true and virtuous girl, and I should not dare to imagine that she could lose herself to the influence of profligate noblemen and hypocritical celebrants.

In that vein, I take to addressing your inquiry concerning your parentage. I have, throughout your life, sought to protect and shield you against your interested relatives, per my oath to your mother before her sad passing. I have also sought to protect you against any reckless behavior which could be aimed towards a father that only partway fulfills his duties to you. The truth is that he _does_ know of you, and for many years he has made to me some small donations of money intended for your upkeep; these I have put aside for your dowry, which shall be a handsome one when the time comes for it to be claimed. However, I advise you against making this information known too readily, lest you attract fortune-hunters and spendthrifts into interested courtships.

I feel that a father who thinks his only duty to a daughter should be to send her guardian an occasional gift of money is a man who has little to either gain or *offer in meeting the said daughter; and I can vouch that he has never made any request to meet with you nor written any letters intended for you in all your eighteen years. I have no wish to poison a daughter against a father, to whom she does owe natural duties of love; but nor do I wish to fill a girl with false hopes or to compel a waste of affection and thought toward a man, who thinks but little of her.*

This being stated, I feel nevertheless that you are of an age where the knowledge of your parentage might be of some benefit to your peace of mind, as well as to any future marriage partner you might gain for yourself. I will thus confide in you the secret, which I trust you shall keep well-guarded and shall reveal only to those who have utter need to know it. Your father is The Marquess of Clarendon, whose personal name I understand to be Francis Montblank. Having written this, I beg you to keep this letter well concealed and never let it fall into the hands of another, lest it be put to some unsavory usage. I suggest that you commit the name to memory, and then burn this paper.

This information being known, I advise that you do nothing more with it. However, if you should find yourself in any need, only let me know of it, my dear Honoria, and I shall be at your disposal.

With blessings,
Your dutiful guardian.

Reading this, Honoria's heart raced at the revelation of a secret which had been kept from her all her life. Her father was a man called Francis Montblank, Marquess of Clarendon. And he was not wholly ignorant of her existence — not even wholly inattentive to it, as Burney admitted he had been supplied with money for her upkeep. While it was a small consideration, it was something.

What Honoria was disappointed not to receive, was any detail of how her father and mother had come to know each other, or had fallen into their situation. It was a subject of some interest to her, for she wondered — was she at risk of falling into a similar pattern? Could she find herself, like her mother, the forgotten dam of some nobleman? She recalled Reverend Burney's warning, "conduct yourself as always, with modesty and integrity and virtue... The Honoria I have always known is a true and virtuous girl, and I should not dare to imagine that she could lose herself to the influence of profligate noblemen and hypocritical celebrants." Burney seemed to trust her judgment enough to declare those encouraging words, but also to mistrust her enough to admit the necessity of their being spoken.

Per the clergyman's instruction, Honoria committed the name of her father to memory, and then — hesitating to do so, wishing all the while that she did not need to do so — she burned the note, so that no unworthy hands should be able to gain this information.

She then decided, upon the next opportunity that she would have to speak with Elizabeth, to inquire about her father. Perhaps

Elizabeth might know something about the Marquess, or about her mother's situation. Honoria had never broached the subject to Elizabeth before, and when upon one afternoon she did so, it was something of a surprise to her.

"You wish to know about your mother and father!" repeated Elizabeth with amazement. It had always been, in her mind, a taboo subject — something one *deliberately* did not discuss.

"Having never met my father, and my mother having died when I was too young to know what went on, I do wonder about them. You are old enough to have known my mother — and perhaps my father, too?"

Elizabeth shook her head. "Your father, I never met. Though your mother and I were close in age to one another, moreso than often befalls an aunt and niece, we did not live in the same city: she was in London, whilst I have lived most of my life in Bath. Your father was a secret that she kept guarded even from her family, and perhaps would not have revealed at all had not your coming into the world necessitated it. That he was a nobleman is all I knew of it; and it was my understanding that he was already wed, or was engaged to be, so that there was no hope of compelling a marriage between your mother and he."

Already this was as much information as Honoria had ever managed to learn about her father. Yet it was as much as there was: Elizabeth genuinely knew nothing more of the subject than that which she had just revealed.

Once she understood that there was nothing more to know, Honoria left off the subject for more pleasant chatter. Yet inwardly she wished, with desperation, to know what had been the cause of her mother's downfall — the same mother who was of good family, the same mother who entrusted her daughter to the careful upbringing of Mr. Burney: what had ever motivated her to forsake all goodness and virtue, and put herself into such a shocking and ruinous state? And what role had her father played in all of it? Was she descended from an immoral rake, or had there been some good intentions on his part that circumstances beyond his control had forced him to abandon?

These questions, to Honoria, were of the utmost importance — for now, as she found herself being courted, she had to wonder what potential might also lie within those men, too? What potential might lie within *herself*? Could *any* of them be trusted to uphold virtue and honesty — even her own person?

By night, staring out the window as a woman left the townhouse of the Viscount next door, Honoria wondered what it was that could drive women to such a state that they could forget their own honor, and could overlook the unhappy consequences that should accompany the loss of that honor.

CHAPTER 4

Public balls were twice weekly at the Bath Assembly Rooms, and Elizabeth invited Honoria to one of these events. Margaret was offended at not being allowed to attend with them, but Elizabeth insisted that she was too young: "When you are 16 you can begin attending public assemblies, but 14 is not old enough to mingle with such a crowd."

Margaret complained the whole time as Honoria and Elizabeth prepared, that she should be permitted to attend as well, but her mother was unmoved and eventually ordered Margaret out of the dressing room if all she was going to do was complain. At last Elizabeth was able to focus all her attentions onto the duties she owed her young cousin. At 36 years old, Elizabeth was just barely old enough that she could have been Honoria's mother, but was not so far removed in age that she could not be perceived as a peer as well. Afterall, if a man of 36 were to propose to her, his age would not likely cast him as an unfit husband.

Honoria, garbed in her new ugly dress and with hair styled to the mode, made her debut at the Assembly Rooms for the weekly Dress Ball. Elizabeth attended as chaperone, and introduced Honoria to those whom she knew. Honoria was a very beautiful girl, and so it was not long that she was left without a partner. In the meantime, Elizabeth secretly, but very astutely, talked with friends about her charge.

"She was my aunt's daughter; her father was a Marquess, someone very wealthy, I understand, though I have not ever had the pleasure of meeting him. She was raised in the country by a good Reverand, and this is her first time into the city..."

The news that the daughter of a Marquess had come to the town was news that spread rapidly amongst the evening's crowd. People who were interested in forming connections took note. Her virtuous upbringing made her all the more seemly as marriage material. Nobility and virtue and beauty in one — how rare and how desirable!

When the event was over, Honoria had enjoyed a lovely time at the ball, and had danced every dance. She had been introduced to a Mr. Elliot, Mr. Roberts, Mr. Willoughby, Mr. Woodbead, and Mr. Lauriston, all fine young men.

On the following day, as was customary, some of these gentlemen came calling at the house of the Everdeens in order to visit again with Honoria. This was something of a surprise to her, as in her experience normally the boys from Derby were not willing to travel so far as to come and see her in Blore the day after a dance. She was kept so busy in entertaining the interested men, that all other plans she had had for the day were abandoned, by necessity.

Mr. Lauriston, who seemed to be the most lofty of the lot, began making some inquiries to Honoria about whether she would be interested in attending another ball at his house in the near future. Honoria agreed that she would be delighted for such an opportunity, and Mr. Lauriston thus promised an invitation would be made out for her.

When dinnertime came, and the men were obliged to depart for their own homes, Honoria was so full with the cakes and teas that had been served as refreshments for the constant gentlemen callers, that she could scarcely eat a bite of the evening meal. In spite of her meager appetite, she enjoyed the mealtime; for the Everdeens seemed excited on her behalf. Edward, pleased by her apparent progress, inquired as to how she was finding the local gentlemen.

"They seem to be very agreeable, so far," said Honoria in reply. "And I have never before found gentlemen so attentive! One of the gentlemen, Mr. Lauriston, has promised to invite me to another ball."

Elizabeth and Edward smiled approvingly — the Mr. Lauriston she had met was the youngest son of a very important family, and his invitation offered her possible introductions to some of the higher ranks of society. Of course, it would all depend on what sort of a party he was going to throw; and this was nothing that the Everdeens could influence. They could only hope the new acquaintance with Mr. Lauriston would prove him to be a valuable friend, and that he was not going to be selfish in pursuing Honoria all for himself, for it was felt certain that with a little luck, she could do much better for herself than a youngest son who would inherit little of his family's wealth or titles.

Honoria was only mildly aware of the plans that the Everdeens had in store for her. She understood that she was in Bath to be introduced to possible marriage partners, and naturally everyone hoped those partners would be of good birth or easy wealth; but she imagined that her successes so far had been due much more to chance than to the deliberate interference of her family. God had a plan for her, was her imagining;

For I know the thoughts that I think toward you, saith the Lord, thoughts of peace, and not of evil, to give you an expected end.

∽.∾

On the following day, Honoria received the invitation to the Lauriston ball; it was a party which was intended as a birthday party for Mr. Lauriston's sister, who was also newly engaged. The elder Lauristons were, on the male side, wealthy but untitled landowners, and on the female side were of noble lineage. If any Lauriston cousins were going to attend this party, there was very good potential for nobility to be in attendance. There were nine days to wait between the date when Honoria received the invite, and the date of the ball itself. Those nine days were spent with all the anxiety one can expect of preparing for a longed-for event. With one successful Bath ball to her credit, Honoria was most eager for another and had every reason to expect a similarly good time.

When the day arrived, Mr. Lauriston himself came in a phaeton to collect Honoria for the party, which was in an old palatial house that had probably been a little ways outside of the town at the time of its construction, but which now sat at the edge of the city. Upon entering, Honoria had in her hands a little box tied with a bow for Miss Lauriston, inside of which was a new lace handkerchief — a perfect little birthday gift. Mr. Lauriston introduced Honoria to his sister, who greeted her warmly. Dancing was not yet started, but Mr. Lauriston then asked Honoria if he could be granted the honor of having the first dance with her. She agreed smilingly, very flattered by the attention.

There was a little time before the dancing was to start. At a private party, everyone was unofficially considered to be introduced, meaning it was acceptable for people to begin talking to one another without having necessarily met before; but as Honoria was acquainted with almost nobody, Mr. Lauriston began to introduce her around to his friends and to anyone he thought might make a good friend to her. He was also very proud to have the gorgeous creature with him as his guest and was secretly hoping for the self-flattery to gain by showing her off. The place was populated with nothing but the kind of people Mr. Burney had dreamed of seeing Honoria introduced to. Her mission was fulfilled. She had made it!

After being introduced to both males and females of quality, all of whom seemed perfectly charmed by Honoria, or "Miss Wright" as she was introduced, the revelers began to line up for the ball. It was summertime and the late-setting sunlight was still coming through the windows; but chandeliers had been lighted all the same and the whole room shone brightly.

The band began to play the first song; Miss Lauriston and her fiancé were the first ones up to dance, as was the custom. Young Mr.

Lauriston and Honoria talked happily as they awaited their turn — it was growing very apparent that Mr. Lauriston had developed a special favoritism to Honoria already, and was perhaps even a little bit in love with her. Honoria, who was made for love, flirted back without qualm, even if she wondered whether Mr. Burney would approve.

Their turn arrived, and the pair began their dance. It was a lively and difficult series of steps, but it was one Honoria had danced before. However, she had never danced it in such a narrow skirt! It seemed like every movement she made was cut short by the limitations of her hem. She had to begin devoting much of her mental powers to simply maintaining her balance, and consequently forget about trying to appear graceful or artistic. Then about 45 seconds in, that which she most feared came to pass — she extended her leg but was caught once again by her skirt, and this time, she was unable to make a save. Honoria fell to the ground in a humiliating stumble, as all the onlookers watched her. She could hear the gasp from the crowd. Her own heart sank as she knew the shame of her tumble; it totally overwhelmed the pain she felt of banging her knees and elbows on the hard floor. This was not a mere slip, this was a full-on whole-body fall to the ground that left her sprawled across the chalked tiles. The musicians, placed in an out of the way spot in the room, could not see the mishap and did not stop their cheerful playing, yet the energy of the horrified crowd surrounded her.

Mr. Lauriston, being responsible for her, quickly checked that she was alright and helped the girl back up to her feet. "Are you alright? Would you like to continue the dance?"

Honoria, with her smarting knees and elbows, and her body quivering with embarrassment, asked to leave the floor. Mr. Lauriston, who was no less embarrassed, agreed and the two of them left at once.

As they passed through the crowd to the repairing room, Honoria could hear a whisper from someone: "She must have had too much to drink."

Honoria's heart sank even further. She had not partaken of any refreshments *whatsoever* at the party, but now *everyone* (for this random whisper was presumed to represent *everyone*) was assuming she was fall-down drunk!

Mr. Lauriston attended to Honoria out of duty, but the fact was that his own estimation of her was suddenly quite shattered by witnessing her ungraceful dancing and the mishap in front of all his friends. He knew it was *he* that would be teased for it later, since it was he who had invited her and introduced her to everyone. He left her in the repairing room — a little room where women who had accidentally torn their garments, or who had danced themselves into near-faints, could wait in privacy to recover or mend their clothing. It was a convenient place to leave her, and after wishing her the best, Mr. Lauriston sulked back out and hoped that she would not reemerge before the next dance was over and his duties to her would be considered complete.

In the repairing room, which was effectively just a large closet, Honoria was close to tears from the shame of her most undignified fall. Just a few minutes before she had been on top of the world, and now she had experienced certain *social death*!

She remained longer than was necessary, trying to regain her composure. A maid who was waiting made some repairs to the hem of her dress, which was beginning to verge on ripping apart at the seams. Honoria was glad to at least be spared from that additional shame, and the maid, seeing that the girl was upset, gave a few reassuring words that whatever accident had befallen on the dance floor would soon be forgotten, and not to let the event spoil her evening.

Somewhat fortified by that promise, Honoria did eventually emerge, with caution, back out among the waiting dancers. By this time Mr. Lauriston was dancing with a new partner. Honoria took a seat and, wide eyed, scanned the room to determine if any people were staring at her or laughing at her.

Indeed, there was one set of eyes that were upon her, and to her embarrassment they met with hers. The gentleman was a young, lean, dark-haired, well-dressed man of approximately 26 years. He smiled at her, and immediately approached her and asked if she would like to dance with him.

Honoria was amazed that she was still getting *any* dance requests after what had happened. She agreed at once, gave her name to the gentleman, and he told her that his name was De Ryall. When their turn came, Honoria danced well enough — this song offered a simple bunch of dainty, unenthusiastic steps that were no obstacle in her fashionable gown. The gentleman was very sweet and understanding towards her, and possessed of such grace and such kindness she could almost have swooned again for how it overwhelmed her. The pair danced astoundingly well, and when the set was over, Honoria was returned to her seat feeling much eased. Perhaps there *was* chance for recovery of her dignity!

She was later to learn that in fact her partner had been *Lord* Rhodophil de Ryall, an Earl in his own right. But for now, Honoria knew only that he was a sweet and pleasant man, who was willing to take her back to the dance floor even after her earlier embarrassment.

After dancing, Lord de Ryall made his way over to the punch bowl, where he took a cup to refresh himself. A friend of his, Lord Charles, began to speak with him. Lord Charles was about 22 years old, blonde, with a sturdy build, with nothing at all objectionable about his appearance, but plenty objectionable about his manners.

"Dancing with that drunken girl, are you?" asked Lord Charles. (For it was he that had made the earlier accusation against Honoria, which she had overheard.)

"I did not perceive her to be drunk in the slightest," answered Lord de Ryall. "She seems a very charming and respectable girl; I believe she merely had a slip on the floor earlier, as could happen to anybody. It was nothing more than bad luck, which engendered her fall."

"I have my doubts on that," said Lord Charles. "She has probably recovered her wits since then, but I have viewed before what a tipsy girl looks like, when hitting the dust."

"Oh, no, I think you are unjust to her. She appears to be in every way sound and intelligent and virtuous."

"I shall take a look at her and discover for myself, then," said Lord Charles, and he finished his punch at once, and then walked out to the sitting area. He approached Honoria with a request to have the next dance with her. Honoria accepted with delight. The pair of them danced gaily, and had only a couple of near-stumbles; but nothing to have been too ashamed about, in her mind.

Honoria's evening did recover, and though she continued to fret in secret that people were judging her or gossiping about her spill on the dance floor, for the most part she was able to have a good time. Mr. Lauriston, having been her ride to the ball, did the courteous thing and took her back to her home at the end of the evening; but his enthusiasm for her was much diminished, and as they bade each other goodnight, he invented an excuse about how he would not be able to pay her the customary follow-up visit, but that she should not read it as any affront. And he afterwards rode back to his house, expecting never to see her again.

CHAPTER 5

The following day, Mr. Lauriston was paying visits to his favorite dance partners of the previous night. Lady Sarah Huysmans, another girl with a courtesy title, was his hostess of the moment. As they happily relived their fun at the party while drinking champagne punch, which Lauriston had spiked with gin, the subject of his embarrassing first dance partner became their talk.

"Who was that girl again?" asked Lady Sarah with a dismissive tone, imbibing her fourth cup of the strong beverage. "Nora-something?"

"Honoria Wright," said Mr. Lauriston with a bit of an eye-roll. "She is tolerably good looking, but it cannot compensate for what a clumsy oaf she is. I should have never brought her to such a gathering — I had met her at a public assembly where, in comparison to *that* crowd, she had appearance of being a bit more of a prize."

"Some sponge out of the country, I take it?" asked Lady Sarah with a laugh. (*Sponge* at this time suggested a person looking to marry for money.)

"Doubtless," answered Lauriston, taking a box of snuff from his pocket. "Although I am led to understand that she is the natural child of someone or another. Clearly little of her father's good breeding was transferred to her." He took a *un pris* of the dark powder through his nose, and offered some to Lady Sarah, who imitated his action. "But let us not talk any more of that — I am really quite embarrassed by the whole event. Let us talk, my dear Lady Sarah, of happier moments in the night, such as those we spent in our fine performance of the reel!"

And those who remembered Honoria from the party generally remembered her in a like manner: an embarrassing moment in an otherwise very merry evening.

Meanwhile at the Everdeen house, over an afternoon breakfast, the family eagerly sought to know how Honoria's time at the party had gone. She was a little reluctant to talk of it, but at last was urged to relate both the good and bad. Elizabeth and Edward tried not to demonstrate dismay with Honoria when she told of the embarrassing accident, but Margaret in her way blurted out:

"How do you fall because of a skirt, can you not walk? Ugh."

Elizabeth scolded Margaret for her rudeness, and Honoria tried to not let on how the insult wounded her afresh.

"It is alright," said Elizabeth with a sigh, secretly wondering if Honoria's accident really did undo any of the apparent progress that before had been made. She gave the standard reassurance nevertheless: "Anyone who obsesses over a little mishap such as that, and holds it against you, is not worthy of your company."

The real test of Honoria's success or failure was to be later in the day, when it would be expected that some of her dance partners might come to visit. There was an unspoken dread that she would be offered no visits: *that* would be the proof that her disgrace at the dance had been a social disaster. The clock hit 2 o'clock, and almost at the stroke of the bell, there was a knock at the door.

The visitors were let inside and it was revealed that they were Lord de Ryall and Lord Charles, both come at the same moment. The two men seemed a little dismayed about each other's presence, like they had not deliberately timed a simultaneous visit; but they were there, and neither was about to let the other get in his visit first.

Honoria received the two men happily, and Elizabeth half chaperoned, half encouraged them. She was pleased to realize that both visitors had titles, even if *Lord Charles* was clearly a courtesy title (but it nevertheless meant that his father was important — either a Marquess or a Duke.) If quality men like these were still talking to Honoria, it indicated that she had not ruined her reputation entirely. Elizabeth held back from prying too much, and left it to Honoria to inquire about the lives of her own beaux.

Nevertheless, Lord de Ryall and Lord Charles were both exceptional men; hardly representative of the general consensus held about Honoria. Amongst the bulk of the partiers she was held with either disdain or indifference; and though the two young lords were acquainted with one another, they were rather different characters to each other. Lord de Ryall was a courteous and virtuous man, who was moved by sympathy after seeing a sweet girl who endured an unfortunate mishap; whereas Lord Charles had perceived a girl who was not too hoity-toity, a country girl, and who might be a bit more fun than the usual stuck-up crowds of Bath. Even after meeting her they had maintained different ideas of her. De Ryall believed she was an honest and upright female who was worthy of being known; and Lord Charles perceived instead a fast and fun party girl who would doubtless show her true colors once he became a little more familiar.

Of course the ways of the world made it impossible for them to simply display this openly to poor Honoria. It was her duty to learn it, by whatever limit means she was offered, and any failure to accurately judge her suitor would be her fault; just as Mr. Lauriston was blamed for Honoria's failings.

Conversation betwixt the three of them went well, and all appeared to have an agreeable visit in spite of the competition. After about an hour — a generous stay by the standards of the time — the two men departed from the house and went their separate ways.

After the visit, Honoria found herself in a bit of an awkward place. It was apparent that she now had two men who both liked her, at the same time. As a female, she possessed limited power over her mates; all she could do was try to attract, or demure. To send someone away would be considered rude, but it was also viewed as bad mannered to show too much favoritism to any particular man. What to do? What to do? To accept the attentions of both seemed to be her only option, and from there, all that decorum could permit was to hope and pray that her affections and their affections would properly mirror one another.

As she contemplated this, she looked out her window and saw another carriage roll up in front of the house next door. A veiled woman got out of it and went inside. On the one hand Honoria thought it shocking and disdainful that any woman would be calling upon a man like that, and in broad daylight no less; but on the other she could not help but envy the woman who seemed to have taken some kind of control over her own romantic life.

A few days passed. Time was wasted at the Everdeen house in the usual womanly pursuits; sewing, examining fashion magazines, reading worthless novels, and writing letters to faraway friends and family. Honoria sent word to Mr. Burney of her adventures and that she had met a few gentlemen, but she decided against naming them to him.

Then the day came where Elizabeth Everdeen suggested to her young cousin that they might go to the famous Pump Room together for some amusement. Much of Bath society attended the Pump Room multiple times in a week, but this was to be Honoria's first visit to the famous location. Honoria thought the offer was a splendid idea, and she went upstairs where she changed into her new walking dress. Thinking she looked well, she went downstairs to await Elizabeth; but when Elizabeth found her, the poor embarrassed woman was forced to explain to Honoria that at the Pump Room, one should dress nearly as well as one might for an evening ball, toned down only with a pelisse or a bonnet attached. Honoria herself felt stupid for not knowing this, thanked God that at least she had learned the requirement before making the blunder of arriving at the location in such a state of undress. She returned to her own room and changed into her second-best gown, the one which formerly had been her best and favorite and which she had worn at the Assembly Rooms the fortnight before. Admittedly, she liked it a lot less with its new narrow skirt and flounces, but it remained her second-best dress. She topped it off with the same bonnet she had meant to wear for walking, and Elizabeth approved of this ensemble.

It had been arranged for a hackney to take them to the Pump Room from the house. It was not a long route, but they were not going to walk it while dressed in ball-gowns! Soon the coach was before the all-important center of Bath's society, and the two females stepped through the great neo-classical columns. The Pump Room was a newly built room — not even a decade old — having replaced an earlier and much smaller space. It was a spacious hall, with high ceilings and walls all painted white. A statue of Beau Nash (who was, effectively, the father of Bath Society) was placed in a recess in one part of the room; up above was a balcony where musicians were playing pleasant tunes. The room was crowded; richly dressed men and women promenaded and socialized, while others lined up by the pump to take the city's famous mineral waters. There were also some less-fashionable folk; genuine sick people who had come to the pumps for medical reasons. A few were even in wheelchairs or on crutches. It was an odd scene to have them all together in one room, though it appeared for the most part that the invalids kept out of the way of the socialites. The general glow of beauty and happiness seemed like it might, nevertheless, be of some additional benefit to the poor sick folk, even if they could not directly participate.

Elizabeth and Honoria paraded through the room multiple times; this was the major activity which one came to do at the Pump Rooms. One was there to be seen. As the two women circled, Honoria glimpsed a person that she thought she recognized. After a couple more passes she was certain of it — Lord de Ryall was in the crowd! However, he looked to be preoccupied, and was part of a large group of other men and women. On the fifth pass Honoria believed that their eyes had met, but as he was so busy with his own party he could do no more than flash her a smile from a distance.

Eventually the women became weary from the promenade, and they decided to take a bit of the Bath waters to refresh themselves. A servant woman handed out glasses poured from the pump, and Elizabeth gave a small tip for the trouble. She then asked Honoria how she liked the event so far, and Honoria indicated she was enjoying herself.

"In that case," said Elizabeth, "I shall sign us up for a subscription to these rooms, so we may return at leisure; the book is here, I shall note us down."

Elizabeth left Honoria behind by the pump as she wove her way through the crowd to enter their names down for Pump Room subscription. By herself, Honoria sought to find some occupation. She looked across the room to see how Lord de Ryall was doing, but he appeared to be paying her little notice, and she did not want to disturb him if he was busy.

Then as she was waiting, an old man on a crutch addressed her. He was friendly, and spoke to her with a country man's honest and straightforward manner. Honoria naturally answered him back as she would have any other friendly countryman. They got to chatting and it was revealed that he actually had recognized Honoria because they were both from the vicinity of Blore; this nice old man, named Robert Thompson, was in Bath on one of the city's charitable plans: for the city of Bath, believing its waters to be genuinely curative for a variety of illnesses, had its own fund that was created to allow poor sick people to come to the city to take the waters and receive medical treatments at no expense, apart from what it would cost them to make the trip itself. Old Mr. Thompson had qualified for this aid on account of his ulcerous stomach. The two got to talking about Blore, how each was finding the city, and such typical topics. It all seemed so natural to Honoria that it did not strike her that others might think it unusual for a well-dressed young lady (standing alone!) to be talking to an old man who couldn't possibly be acquainted with her; or if he were an acquaintance, it reflected poorly on her own social position. When Elizabeth returned and saw the two in conversation together, she was forced to swiftly but politely put an end to their merry talk. She delayed explaining her reasoning to Honoria until after they had left the Pump Rooms.

When Honoria learned about her *faux pas*, she was torn between whether she ought to be embarrassed by her behavior and hope that no one had seen her, or whether she should be perturbed that Bath was full of people as could not merely observe a young female talking to a poor, sick old man from her hometown without thinking ill of it.

CHAPTER 6

The Sydney Garden Vauxhall was designed to compete with the famous Vauxhall gardens of London, and though their scale was smaller, the bored paraders of Bath were almost equally satisfied by it. In summer, concerts, fireworks and other entertainments were routinely held in that location, and it was to one of these events that Elizabeth brought her family and Honoria, one pleasant evening.

It was a garden in the sense of being a green spot — a rare thing in a time when trees were more valued for firewood than decoration. The Sydney Garden was a space consisting of mostly grass, a few trees, a few flower bushes; a park, by the modern definition. It was done in the naturalistic Capability Brown fashion; by the standards of the time is was a very fancy and even somewhat exotic space, containing water and bridges in imitation of Chinese styles that were normally only seen painted on imported teacups, as well as a maze clipped from some hedges, of which finding the center would be rewarded with the chance to try out a fantastic gadget called a Merlin's Swing.

On this evening, in the garden, a little string quartet was playing some popular tunes for the public. There would be a fireworks show later in the night, but at this time the sun had barely set and the sky was still alight with orange and yellow.

The Everdeens, plus Honoria, began the parade around the greenery, looking for familiar faces, and taking in the scenes. Some lights were being put out by liveried servants of the groundskeeper, to keep the gardens in brightness. After wandering some time, enjoying the view, Honoria thought she witnessed some familiar faces amidst the glow of the lamps. They were people she had met at the birthday gathering of Miss Lauriston the month before. As she got closer, she recognized among the friendly faces the one belonging to Lord Charles. He made eye contact with her and seemed to beckon her. Honoria convinced the Everdeens to approach him, and she was able to greet the fair young aristocrat.

"Miss Wright, how fortunate I am to see you here," said Lord Charles in a respectably flat tone that mitigated his enthusiasm. Honoria felt her heart grow warm at the compliment, nonetheless.

Lord Charles invited Honoria to join his party, and with the blessing of the Everdeens she separated from them, and took the arm of Lord Charles, her new escort for the night. Agreements were made that Lord Charles could host her amongst his friends, and then have the honor of seeing her home at the end of the night.

It was an exciting yet worrisome moment for Honoria — she had only really met Lord Charles twice, once when he danced with her at the Lauriston ball, and the other when he had come to visit her the day after. But he was a respectable man, and of good birth, and there was every reason, from her viewpoint, to assume that he could be entrusted with her safety. They bade farewell to the Everdeens, and Honoria had all expectation of a pleasant night with Lord Charles and his company of friends.

Yet it seemed that hardly were the Everdeens out of sight, when Lord Charles seized Honoria by the hand and began to run from the group with her, tugging her along with him into the darkness. At first, in confusion, she thought it might be some kind of game and that the rest of the party would come following with them; but it took only a moment to see that Lord Charles was dragging her off alone. His destination seemed to be a darkened area of trees, somewhat out of sight.

Realizing his intentions, Honoria cried out and refused to take another step. "Good heavens!" she cried, "What way are you going?"

"To where," answered he, "we shall be the least observed!"

Astonished, Honoria declared she would go no further. "Turn us back to the party!" she demanded.

"And for what, my angel?" he said in a tone that seemed to be utterly uncaring to her concerns.

Honoria's heart beat with resentment. With the entirety of her strength she pushed him away and wrenched her arm from him. Lord Charles nearly fell backward at the force of it. Seeming as if genuinely perplexed, he demanded to know what was wrong.

"What is *wrong*?" cried Honoria, amazed at such a question. "How dare you to treat me with such insolence?"

"Insolence!" repeated he.

"Yes, Lord Charles, insolence; from you, from whom I had received a promise for protection; not for such treatment as this."

"By Heaven," cried he, in a fiery tone, "you amaze me. Why, tell me — why else do I see you here, and seeking out my company?"

Honoria was both offended and outraged by his words. "Why? To become better acquainted with a gentleman whom I had reason to *think* I could grow fond of, whom I had reason to *think* should offer pleasant company, and whom I had to reason to *think* was worthy of the designation of gentleman! If anything I have said has caused you to believe that it was any wish on my part to spend an evening with you in the bushes, you can be certain that such a statement was taken quite in error of its intention!" Angrily, she turned away from him; and started her return to the part of the garden where she beheld that lights and company awaited. Lord Charles began to follow her, in a confused silence as if he were truly unsure of what to say.

"For shame, sir!" she continued in a compound of woe and indignation, "do you suppose that you can urge me by these means? Do you take advantage of the absence of my friends to insult me?"

"Not at all, Madam," cried he. "I would sooner forfeit my life than fall to such depths. But you have flung me into such amazement. I will confess, I expected no such displeasure from you."

Honoria was not even sure what to say in response to such a remark. "How could you possibly think such action could please me?"

The answer was a complicated one, and such as was not worthy of being spoken at a time such as this; and he was intelligent enough to know that it would provide her no comfort even then. Instead he did all that was in his power, and actually flung himself at her feet, as if careless as to whomever might see him, proclaiming, "Oh, Miss Wright — loveliest of women — forgive me — I beseech you forgive me! If I have offended, if I have insulted you — I could kill myself at the thought!"

Honoria made no answer; but quickening her pace walked on silently and sullenly. Lord Charles leapt after her, then snatched her hand with violence, and began to beg her forgiveness. He did it with such earnestness of supplication, that, merely to escape his importunities, she was ultimately forced to grant the pardon he requested; though it was accorded with a very ill grace and only halfheartedly. Inwardly Honoria knew she would not truly dismiss this moment from her memory no matter how she promised that she could forgive and forget.

"But we must return immediately to your party," said Honoria. "Or I shall revoke my forgiveness; it is only granted on condition that we return immediately and there be no more of these antics from you."

"Antics from me!" cried Lord Charles, with a tone of indignation; but knowing Honoria would not overlook any further delay, he granted her request and returned to the party.

When they rejoined with their friends, there were some newcomers waiting in the group that had not been thereamongst before their departure. One of the new arrivals was Lord de

Ryall. When Honoria and Lord Charles entered together from some nearby bushes, de Ryall observed them, and looked at the scene with a recognizable expression of concern. Honoria observed it and her face colored immediately with embarrassment. She wondered if de Ryall rightly interpreted her shame to stem from the possibility of untoward behavior being assumed upon her, when she had done nothing wrong, or if he wrongly would interpret it as born of being caught at actual untoward behavior, which had not occurred but might be imagined.

Since Lord Charles was technically her guardian for the night, as well as her promised means home for the evening, Honoria hesitated to leave his presence no matter how badly she wished to. But after seeing his behavior she was also become wary of him, and she took to concealing herself in the centers of crowds, and sought to talk to others so that Lord Charles could not opportunely pull her away again.

Her evasion of Lord Charles ultimately led her to lock herself into conversation with Lord de Ryall, who seemed uneasy about speaking to her yet did not seem unwilling. Honoria was left to wonder at his behavior, while subjecting him to her attention lest she be in danger of some new scheme from Lord Charles.

Lord de Ryall himself was cautious about speaking with Honoria, because he sought to smoke out precisely what was the nature of her relationship with Lord Charles. He had no way of knowing whether she had been meeting Lord Charles during the several weeks since last he saw them together, after the Lauriston dance, and no way of knowing what the two of them had been doing alone before (re)joining into their group some moments before. If she was being seriously courted by Lord Charles, he did not wish to infringe. Honoria had often been on his mind since their meeting, but he would force himself to forget her if her heart already was pledged to some other man.

The fair Honoria was now chatting away about the charms of her old home in the countryside, and Lord de Ryall was paying due attention, yet his mind kept drifting away to that subject of what was her situation with Lord Charles. It was a question he might ask of Lord Charles directly; yet he did not trust that he would receive any truthful answer from him: Lord Charles clearly was in pursuit of Honoria for himself, and might either exaggerate his success out of pride, or outright lie in order to discourage any rivals. No, the information would need to come from Honoria.

Seeking to combine courage with tact, he was able to bring himself to ask of her whether she had been making any new friends or acquaintances since coming to the city?

"Oh, indeed I have!" Honoria answered. "Why, there was Mr. Lauriston, and it need not be said, you."

"Is that all?" said de Ryall, his heart beating hopefully. "I should have wished you to have a mob of willing suitors and many warm friendships by this time."

Honoria might have wished it too, but she understood why it had not come. "I think that my accident at Miss Lauriston's birthday did my reputation some harm. It is very peculiar what it takes here, in Bath, to damage a reputation or not."

"Indeed," said de Ryall. "I recall that Lord Charles and I were quite concerned by it, at the time."

"Oh, that Lord Charles!" said Honoria, not willing to use any stronger pejorative than the word *that*. "He has been behaving most disagreeably this evening. I ordered him to return me post-haste to to this party, after he had sought to drag me away."

"So then, you *are* here with Lord Charles?" asked de Ryall, barely able to contain the alarm this information provoked in him.

"Indeed," said Honoria, not wishing to appear glum or upset by the situation yet also longing to make it known that she was not happily attached. "He had made an offer to see me home after the fireworks tonight."

"Where do you live?"

"In Broad Street."

De Ryall did not like the sound of that. A carriage ride to take place between a lone man and woman, at this time in history, was permissible; but just as in modern times it is allowed for a man and woman to be alone in a car together, it is understood there can be dangers in such an arrangement. Even a distance as short as Broad Street could present her with danger. It sounded as if Lord Charles had already tried to take advantage of Honoria's dependence upon him once already this night — would it be wise to allow him another opportunity?

De Ryall set his brain to work. Was there any way that Honoria could honorably back out of an offer she had already accepted, in order to take up another? Of course she was in her rights to accept or reject whatever offers she wanted, but rights and manners did not always fall upon the same groove.

About this time the green men came out, and began to light the fireworks throughout the park. Roman candles began sparkling near the canal, and after that, several larger rockets were shot off in the more open realms of the vauxhall. Watching together, Honoria and de Ryall were caught up in amazement, and as one their hearts jumped at an explosion of light here and thrilled at a fountain of sparks blasting there.

As if by an instinct the pair clasped hands, lost in the moment; but as soon as Honoria realized what she did, she drew her hand away in shame. De Ryall was disappointed but still understanding of the reasons why. He comprehended her genuine behavior, ever artless, ever honest; and she was drawn to the boundless understanding and kindness which he seemed to display. The delightful sparks before them excited their spirits and intensified the connection between them. Honoria nearly felt as if her heart could burst. She turned toward de Ryall, and their gaze connected. The mutual glance was too much for Honoria: for what it made her wish to do would have sullied her forever in her own esteem.

CHAPTER 7

When the fireworks were done, de Ryall was still occupied with the matter of how to rescue Honoria from the destined carriage ride home with Lord Charles. It struck de Ryall that he could make a slight breach of etiquette himself, for Honoria's sake, and could begin to *insist* that she allow him to take her home, such that Lord Charles would not be able to pressure Honoria into keeping her promise without putting her into an embarrassing spot, which (it was hoped) Lord Charles would be too decent to do, especially under the watching eyes of others.

Not many revellers were anxious to hurry home after the fireworks, and the party of good company into which Honoria had been brought was now cheerily passing time in talks, walks, and use of the swings which were posted about the gardens. Brave girls who were unconcerned by their skirts being blown back consented to sit down on the rope and board swings and to let their beaux push them as high as they could go. Honoria was not among them, although Lord Charles did extend such an invitation to her.

Honoria was too caught up with Lord de Ryall and his attention to make much note of their surroundings. They were in a lovely night-time park with friends, but they could have been on the moon or in a sewer for all she really sensed. Her eyes were locked upon Lord de Ryall's, and his full concern was upon her.

Lord Charles was coming to notice this, and it was irritating to him. How could the sweet Honoria cast him off, protesting modesty, and then proceed to flirt so openly with Rhodophil de Ryall? He approached Honoria, making every endeavor to conceal his annoyance, and informed her that it was time they should be going. "I have promised your cousins that I should see you safely home," he said.

Lord de Ryall knew what to do, and enacted his own plan. "Oh, my! I have been insisting to Miss Wright that she should allow *me* the pleasure of seeing her home — have I not, Miss Wright? Surely you will not deny me such a heartfelt pleasure."

Lord de Ryall had not been able to discuss his scheme with Honoria, and he could only hope that she understood what he was trying to do.

"Indeed," said Lord Charles, appealing to Honoria and trying all the harder to conceal his aggravation, "the pleasure will be all mine, and although I do comprehend this gentleman's enthusiasm and wishes, I do believe that it is *I* that your family *expects* to see you home."

Lord de Ryall appealed all the harder. "And it pains me so, to deprive another of your companionship, and yet I do think it will be found much more pleasant in my own coach. It has been newly refurbished and will be a most comfortable ride."

"And what greater honor I can grant you with a ride in mine," said Lord Charles, now snidely breaking good manners, "for though Lord de Ryall comes only in his own coach, emblazoned with the arms of the Earls de Ryall; I have come this night in the coach of the Marquess of Clarendon and with all the honors that entails."

"The Marquess of Clarendon!" parroted Honoria, wondering how the two men could be connected. This new development had an instantaneous influence upon her, and suddenly, even the promise of safety offered by Lord de Ryall seemed less intriguing than the possibility of mystery uncovered.

"Well," Honoria said, "I suppose as I have provided *you* the prior claim, I am obliged to choose your company above the generosity of Lord de Ryall; though I hope you both understand me, that I am most grateful for each of your offers."

Lord de Ryall felt his heart drop. Honoria would be going home with his rival! What could have possibly urged her to such a decision? In the back of his mind he made a note that the mention of the Marquess seemed to have turned her in Charles's favor, but for now he was more worried and upset to see her heading off into the darkness of the night with that man, who was shadier than any midnight street.

De Ryall's first thought was that he might be able to have his own coach follow Lord Charles's, in order to be sure of her safety, but in the crush of horses, vehicles and sedans waiting to pick up the wealthy garden subscribers from their summer evening, there looked like little hope for success in that endeavor. He watched with sadness as Lord Charles and Honoria climbed into the former's family coach, and the horses began to slowly work their way out onto the streets.

The route to the Everdeen's home was simple one: from the Sydney Gardens it was a straight jot down Great Pultney Street, then a right turn onto Broad Street, upon which the house was to be discovered. It was a 15 minute ride at its worst.

Honoria first seated herself within the coach, while Lord Charles relayed his instructions to the driver, after which he got in. The vehicle set off very slowly, while Lord Charles began to engage Honoria in some pleasant conversation. As they talked of unimportant subjects, Honoria halfway noticed the lack of lights out the window, but not being familiar with Bath at night thought nothing much of it. Conversation about recent activities, and activities that might be later done, continued throughout, but Honoria was actually trying to steer the topic back to that important subject of the Marquess of Clarendon.

"So earlier you had mentioned that you *know* the Marquess of Clarendon?"

"I do, but let us not talk of that," said Lord Charles with a tone of irritation.

"Why not? Has he done something to offend you?" asked Honoria with great interest.

"Have you some romantic interest in *him*, now?" asked Lord Charles, failing to conceal anything about his current mood. He was jealous and annoyed at Honoria, and how she seemed always to want to talk of any man but himself.

Acknowledging his annoyance, Honoria backed off the subject. "I did not mean to offend you, sir. I simply have heard a little about the Marquess and had wished to know more. If it is too unpleasant a subject, however, I will urge you no further toward talk of it." In her mind she wondered what the Marquess could have done to Lord Charles to make him feel negatively towards him. But her mind was not long upon this; for it was at about this point, that Honoria realized they should be nearing Broad Street — and yet, when she looked out the window of the coach, she saw only moonlit landscape of grass and trees and hills. This was definitely not the center of Bath!

"Goodness! Where are we?" asked Honoria, very alarmed.

Lord Charles looked out the window and seemed less than surprised at what he saw. "Why, the coachman must have misunderstood my instruction. No matter — I am certain that this road will swing round and take us into the city afresh. Enjoy the ride, then, my dear Miss Wright; for such fair and moonlit landscapes are not to be found within the city."

He then rose from his seat and placed himself beside her. Honoria felt her heart sink with fear. It struck her that this "mistake" of the coachman may well have been a deliberate scheme by Lord Charles to take her into isolation. She did not dare think too hard about his possible reasons why; she was only struck with an immediate terror.

Lord Charles then reached out to take her by the hand. Honoria was resistant, and he marked it. He began by making many complaints of her unwillingness to trust herself with him, and begged to know whatever could be the reason for her unease. Honoria did not want to speak aloud the worrying thoughts in her mind, lest they either offend him and produce an unpleasant outrage, or worse — that they might give him *ideas*.

"I am only concerned that my friends might be awaiting me home," she replied. "I do not wish to keep the Everdeens in suspense."

"Oh, Miss Wright," he said soothingly, while taking her hand in his, "if you knew how readily I would dedicate to you not only the present, but all the future time allotted to me! To me, it is a blessing to spend such time with you, and yet you think only of how it might inconvenience your friends?"

"I know only I should not like to be in their place, and be worried for me," she replied.

"What need is there for worry?" he asked. "They know who I am. You do not doubt my honor, do you?"

This was not said rhetorically: he really appeared to be awaiting her answer. Honoria was forced to give her assurance that she trusted him entirely, even though it was completely opposite to what she felt. Again, the truth might prove too inspirational to him.

"I know not why I worry so," said Honoria, "but only that I wish us to return to the city immediately!" She would have liked to pull her hand away from his, and made subtle attempts to do so; but in vain, for he actually grasped it between both of his own moist palms, without any regard to her resistance.

"And does this little moment," he declared, "which is the first of true happiness I have ever known — does it already appear so very long to you? Can you be so cruel as to deny me this pleasure of your too-brief companionship? I could spend lifetimes by your side without it seeming long." And so saying, he passionately kissed her hand. Not a respectable quick kiss, but rather like he was about to eat it.

Honoria could not pretend anymore that she was without fear. She broke forcibly from him, and, putting her head out of the window, called aloud to the coachman:

"Stop this instant! I must get out!"

They were on desolate piece of road, with the city still in view. The coach was on land amidst some hills near a stone quarry, and a little village called Bath Hampton in near sight. No person was about, or else Honoria should have called for assistance. She began endeavoring to open the door. The coachman stopped as he had been instructed, but Lord Charles pulled Honoria back into the box. She let out a cry.

"Miss Wright, what *is* the matter with you?" he asked earnestly. "Calm yourself, there is nothing to fear here. You are quite safe in the coach — safer here than you should be outside at this time of night."

"Then," demanded Honoria, dread in her voice, "take me this instant back to the city. If you do not intend to murder me, for mercy's sake, for pity's sake, *let me get out!*"

"Compose your spirits, my dearest," cried he, "and I will do everything you would have me to." He then called to the coachman himself, and instructed him to turn the coach around and hurry right away to Broad Street. "This stupid fellow," said Lord Charles to Honoria, "has certainly mistaken my orders; but I hope you are now fully satisfied."

Honoria made no answer. She only kept her face to the window, watching which way they drove, but without taking any comfort as she herself was quite unacquainted with either the right or the wrong way.

Lord Charles now poured forth abundant protestations of honor, and assurances of respect, entreating her pardon for having caused any offense, and beseeching her good opinion: but she was quite silent, dreading too much what might happen were she to make reproaches, and bearing too much anger to speak without making them. He asserted that the whole misadventure had only been a result of the driver's error and that he had done nothing to warrant her displeasure. "Miss Wright, please, I beg you to hold no anger towards me. Do not blame me for an honest mistake."

She remained with arms folded and only looking out the window. The city lights were approaching and she could see the Sydney Gardens ahead.

"Miss Wright," Lord Charles continued, "I hope at that least that you shall not wrong me by spreading any talk of this misadventure. It was no fault of mine, I can own to you."

Honoria shot at Lord Charles a most malevolent glare. "Lord Charles, I shall fulfill your wish upon one condition only. I shall never speak of this again, if I be granted the pleasure of never *seeing* you again, leaving me thus with no reason to speak."

"Oh, fair lady!" cried Lord Charles. "How can you pain me with such a demand?"

"How can *you* pain *me* with such?" replied Honoria.

"How! Because I am innocent and would not have falsities circulated."

"Do you imagine that I should gossip so?" cried Honoria. She looked out the window and finally recognized that they were upon the junction of Broad Street. She felt the first flush of relief she had known for an hour.

"In which case, do I have your oath of silence?"

Honoria let out an exasperated sound. "Yes, but you must release me, this instant."

Lord Charles hastily agreed, albeit with expressions of hope that she might be moved to alter her opinions of him in the future. Soon the coach was stopped upon Broad Street, and in the customary way Lord Charles ushered Miss Honoria Wright to the door of her house.

To her utter surprise, there was a male figure waiting near the step. This lurker, she realized, was none other than Lord de Ryall!

Both Honoria and Lord Charles were surprised at seeing him there. Then, suddenly,

Lord Charles broke out in a smile and began to laugh.

"How now! I can quite perceive your reason for being so anxious to return home!" he exclaimed, directing his words to Honoria.

Honoria felt pained at a doubly embarrassing situation — that Lord Charles should think she had a man waiting for her at the house, and that Lord de Ryall should certainly know how long she and Lord Charles had been away.

But without any hesitation, Lord de Ryall made his reply. "Why, Miss Wright, how surprising to find you here! I am only come to visit my friend, who lives in this house." He proceeded then to walk up the stairs of the neighboring townhouse, and to knock, showily, upon the door of the Viscount.

Lord Charles narrowed his eyes at Lord de Ryall, doubting his story; but as he and Honoria walked to her door, a servant did answer at the Viscount's and allow Lord de Ryall to enter.

Honoria watched this with a new consternation. Did Lord de Ryall actually know such an unsavory creature as the Viscount?

Once she was finally inside of her own house, she proceeded straight to her room, bewildered by the events of the night. Had there been some genuine mistake between Lord Charles and his driver? Had Lord de Ryall been waiting to see that she was safely home, or was he truly a friend of that dreadful Viscount next door? And how did Lord Charles know the Marquess of Clarendon, who was her father (Wasn't he? Or had she in some confusion misremembered the name? She suddenly wished that she had not destroyed Mr. Burney's letter, that she might double-check it.)

She took little sleep that night, and what she had was filled with upsetting dreams that only reminded her of these same questions.

CHAPTER 8

Honoria kept her word, and said nothing to Elizabeth or Edward of the late-night carriage ride with Lord Charles. It was an incident she preferred to forget, and there was too much confusion about everything that had happened in the course of the night for her to feel secure in hating or loving the actions of anybody. She did mention to Elizabeth how Charles had tried to pull her away into some darkened area — that was something she had not promised any silence about. Elizabeth and Edward looked concerned at the story, and Margaret replied:

"You should have just slapped that rake till he was bruised as black as the night itself, and walked yourself home."

Honoria smiled a little at the visual. Margaret was young and far from well-mannered, but indeed, Honoria could not envision that Margaret would have politely allowed things to degenerate as far as she herself had done. Perhaps there was value in tossing away manners?

Ah, but then — the only reason she had particularly allowed Lord Charles to drive her home at all was that he had been riding in the carriage of the Marquess of Clarendon. She wondered how these two men might know each other. She questioned to herself: What kind of person might a Marquess permit to let ride in his own coach?

Then she remembered. Charles was his Christian name — unlike Lord de Ryall, "Lord Charles" was a courtesy title; and the only men who received such courtesy titles were the sons of Dukes, or of Marquesses.

Could it be that Lord Charles was the son of the Marquess of Clarendon? And if so, would that not mean that he was her half-brother? The thought made her groan aloud. Everything about her world seemed topsy-turvy. Secret brothers! Secret carriage rides! Secret meetings with meritless Viscounts!

"Is something wrong, Honoria?" asked Elizabeth, hearing the noise she had made.

Honoria assured that she was fine, but in a tone of voice that betrayed her distress. Elizabeth put it down to continued annoyance about Lord Charles's behavior.

"Do not fret yourself with that man," said Elizabeth. "In a way, it is good that you had such an adventure, for now you know his character and also might be saved from like situations to come."

Honoria could immediately hear the words of Psalm 37 run through her brain: *Fret not thyself because of evildoers, neither be thou envious against the workers of iniquity. For they shall soon be cut down like the grass, and wither as the green herb. Trust in the Lord, and do good; so shalt thou dwell in the land, and verily thou shalt be fed. Delight thyself also in the Lord: and he shall give thee the desires of thine heart. Commit thy way unto the Lord; trust also in him; and he shall bring it to pass. And he shall bring forth thy righteousness as the light, and thy judgment as the noonday.*

She tried to take these words to heart. Trust in the Lord, and all would be well. Do good, and all needs would be fulfilled.

Reminded of these duties, Honoria took this as an opportunity to write to Mr. Burney, and tell him of her situation. In order to maintain her oath to Lord Charles, she did not use his name in her letter, nor any other identifying information including her suspicion of blood ties, although she told readily of everything he had done; and using the pseudonym "Lord Rivers" she reported also on Lord de Ryall, and how he had behaved so well until he was discovered in the presence of the wicked viscount.

As per usual, the letter took a few days to reach Mr. Burney, and his response required a few days more; but it came at last to the girl's eager hands, and it read:

My dearest Honoria,

I had hoped to hear of easier times for you in Bath. Notwithstanding the protections offered by Mrs. Everdeen, it appears that the danger to which I had feared subjecting you, now has made its intrusion. Alas, the city is not a place of morality, and many gentlemen are called such only for their birth, rather than out of any deserts. Your friend from the vauxhall should not be regarded as a friend of any sort, and for the sake of modesty, decency, and your virginity all acquaintance with him must be terminated. As to your Lord Rivers, though his intentions may be to the greater honor, and his actions toward you commended, his choice of friends reveals him to lack integrity and virtue, and he too should be avoided and discouraged from your company.

You have some time remaining for your visit in Bath, and I encourage you make use of it to your utmost power. Seek out friends, and with the help and guidance of your cousins and your duties to God, I urge you to seek only such men as are worthy of Honoria. "But they that wait upon the Lord shall renew their strength; they shall mount up with wings as eagles; they shall run, and not be weary; and they shall walk, and not faint."

The clock was ticking. Elizabeth suggested that Honoria might like to attend another of the balls at the Assembly Rooms, as she had experienced there such unequalled success. Honoria's enthusiasm for this whole experiment of matchmaking was very much on the wane, but she agreed to go. This occasion was to take them to one of the weekly fancy dress balls — in other words, a masquerade.

Costumes for these events tended toward the operatic — nobody wanted to wear an unflattering, cheap or undignified outfit. A costume shop was located in town, and Elizabeth and Honoria took a visit there to select masks and such fanciful accessories as were needed. Elizabeth came out with a simple costume of a feathered, bird-like mask — a nice enough thing for a chaperone to wear without drawing too much attention. Honoria, however, needed flash. Elizabeth tried to urge her toward a Cleopatra costume or a gown made up as a splendid representation of the stars and seven planets; but Honoria, lacking Elizabeth's flair and creativity, had wanted to wear a simple Columbine outfit: it was effectively nothing more than a regular lady's dress with an added ruff collar and a small black domino mask. She was able to get her way, and to the ball she donned the simple but appropriate ensemble of the *soubrette*.

The ball was much more crowded than the previous one she had attended at the Rooms. Did the people of Bath simply prefer the fancy dress balls? Or was there some other reason for the heavy attendance?

It was considered good manners for the aristocracy to attend an occasional public assembly: it was seen as a kind of proof that they did not consider themselves too much above the common people. Parliament had let out about six weeks before, and even those who had not immediately departed from London had all made the journey to Bath by now. Yet with everybody in strange masks and garments, it was difficult to tell only at a glance who was whom.

As she scanned the room and looked for familiar faces, she spotted Lord de Ryall floating in the mix. He was dressed as a Spaniard, with a net cap and tasseled breeches. He did not appear to observe her right away, and was instead talking with some friends. He seemed to have so many friends! From viscounts to misters, everybody seemed to like him. Could it really be a sign of poor character that he was friends with everybody?

No sooner had Honoria sat down with Elizabeth, than she was approached by a man in a somewhat reveali108ng satyr's costume, complete with face paint. To his request for a dance she agreed automatically, not realizing that his having addressed her without introduction meant they *did* know one another. It was not until they were back on the floor that she realized, with horror, that she was with Lord Charles!

It was not apparent whether Charles had understood that she did not recognize him when she accepted, but he delighted in having her to himself for the next two dances all the same. "Have you then forgiven me for the mishap with the carriage?" he asked boldly.

Honoria would have liked to slap him, and remembered Margaret's recommendation that she do so — but she kept her calm and said nothing to him at all, and only went through the motions of their dance. She of course had plenty that she would like to say, but how on earth could she possibly voice the things that ran through her mind? Was there even a consensus on the right etiquette for asking if you might be secret half-siblings?

"Surely you are not going to allow this entire dance to pass without speaking to me?" asked Lord Charles, noting her silence.

"I am sorry. How is your *father*?" she asked. Her curiosity on the subject was, of course, genuine, but not till it was past her lips did she think it might sound like a deliberate slight, and she was pleased when she realized it had sounded so, even if in an unintentioned way.

"My father is quite well," replied Sir Charles, disappointed in her response but taking whatever he could get from her, for now. "He continues to be married to my mother. Why this focus upon him? Are you some kind of interested sponge?" Then he brightened, thinking *that* must be the reason why. "Yes. Interested in my family's fortune and titles, are we not?"

"Quite," answered Honoria, not caring at all what he might read into it. She was giving up on fighting him. Let him think whatever he wanted!

Lord Charles laughed, believing that at last he had figured out Honoria's motivations. He was also delighted at what he perceived as her upfront honesty about it. "Slinking away from me because I am a younger son, I suppose? More interested in that Lord de Ryall and what he might offer you?"

"I *am* interested in your family, or else I would not ask. Tell me of them."

Lord Charles indulged her, and spoke of his father's great fortune and holdings, making sure to mention that although he was not heir to the title of Marquess or the associated lands, his father did have a considerable private fortune, a portion of which he should one day enjoy.

"That is pleasant to hear. And what sort of lineage is your family? Is it an old title?"

Lord Charles was amused that she seemed to be so snobbishly worldly, after all her innocent affectations. He told how his father's title went back almost two centuries, and his mother was of continental descent.

"How well do you get on with your father? Is he anything like you?"

Honoria's heart nearly stopped when Lord Charles suggested she could find out for herself

— he offered to introduce them, after the dance. She was dumbstruck, and knew not how to answer. When the dance they had stood up for ended, Lord Charles came with her back to Elizabeth, per the custom. Elizabeth greeted him politely but, remembering Honoria's tale of how he acted at the vauxhall, regarded him with displeasure. She assumed that Honoria had only accepted his offer to dance in polite duty, and that she must be anxious to get away from him. Trying to fulfill her part as a chaperone, Elizabeth suggested to Honoria that they might sit out the second dance of the set and take some refreshments together so as not to grow exhausted (with her real intention being to save Honoria from another dance with him.) To her surprise, Honoria refused, and soon was eagerly back upon the floor with Lord Charles.

Elizabeth was not the only one perplexed by what she saw. From another part of the dance floor, Lord de Ryall observed Honoria and Lord Charles together, with an apparent energy of enthusiasm glowing between them. He was aghast. Could there be a mistake in what he saw? Or had Honoria changed her mind about Lord Charles? Anything was possible at a public assembly, and he tried to reassure himself that Honoria was only dancing with him out of duty for having been asked by that duddering rake. Yet, the look on her face indicated an enjoyment — like she was not merely *forced* to endure it, but *glad*. Lord de Ryall was growing so distracted that his current partner, one Miss Burnistoun, complained that he was not paying attention to her conversation. He apologized, and tried harder to focus upon her despite visions of Honoria flashing through his mind.

During the second dance, Honoria asked more questions about Lord Charles's family, and ignored any remarks he made about her apparent gold-digging. She was beyond caring what he thought, and only worried about what she could learn from him. He tolerated her importune questions, believing they were a sign that he had won her over at last.

When their set ended, Honoria returned to her seat and waited for the next person to ask her for a dance. Elizabeth, however, chose to inquire about her attitude towards Lord Charles.

"Has there been some change in your feelings toward him?" she asked.

"Yes," answered Honoria, telling the truth. But she was hesitant to explain any further — there were still pieces of doubt in her mind and in a way she was ashamed of her behavior, even if she knew she was acting correctly for what she was planning. Her feigned interest in Lord Charles had won her a promise of an introduction to the Marquess — she needed only to wait for it at the end of the ball. Public assemblies did not last all night as did private dances; she had only couple more hours to fill before she would know of her success.

Across the room, Lord de Ryall began making his way towards Honoria, hoping to ask her for the next dance; yet before he could arrive, he saw the Master of Ceremonies approach her, and introduce her to some young man dressed like a Pierrot. How could a Columbine resist a Pierrot? The two of them stood up for the next set, and Lord de Ryall was forced to seek a partner elsewhere. This situation repeated itself many times through the evening — she was proving a most popular dance partner. The fact was that her growing reputation as a drunken party girl who would run off into the bushes at the vauxhall, was providing her with popularity of a sort, even if it was perhaps not the marriage-minded that now sought her out.

By the end of the night, all the dances were danced, and Lord de Ryall was dismayed to find that he had not been able to dance, or even speak with her at all. He left, feeling disappointed with the outcome of his night despite having stood up to every dance that took place.

Honoria was very anxious for the end of the dance, as Lord Charles had promised that it would be the time when her introduction to the Marquess should take place. She approached him near the door — he seemed as if he had intended to leave without remembering his promise, and she had to remind him of it.

"Oh, yes!" he proclaimed. "He is not here tonight — I had meant that you might meet him if you consent to visit with me again some other time. Do you?"

Honoria's heart sank. She had been very much looking forward to ending her night with a meeting of her natural father. Lord Charles had likely been deliberately manipulating her again, in order to compel her to visit with him some more. She agreed to his terms, with reluctance; and he kissed her hand farewell, promising he would call upon her the next day.

CHAPTER 9

The morning after the ball, Honoria made it clear to the Everdeens that if anyone came calling for her, for the traditional post-dance visits, she was to be considered *not at home*. A night of reflection upon Lord Charles's deeds had turned from mere disappointment into a fiery outrage at his action. She suspected he had purposely misled her again. Could that wastrel truly be her half-brother? She wondered how it might influence his behavior towards her if he knew of their relationship — certainly there would be no more carriage rides into the darkness. But would he become nicer in general?

After breakfast, she locked herself into her library-bedroom so as not to be observed if anyone did come calling. True, there had been some others with whom she had danced at the ball, but she was in no good humor for entertaining any of them; and none of them had seemed very impressive, to her. She figured they would simply leave cards. In the meanwhile she endeavored to occupy herself with reading from badly-written novels about even worse heroines in domestic peril, but she found them too much like her own life to be any comfort. Next she turned to her Bible, a good read, and one that Mr. Burney would have approved. She set the book in her lap, opened it, and let the pages fall where they might. She had found herself amidst the psalms. Those were just about the right speed for her; being nothing but prayers to God for comfort, reassurances of God's mercy, or that God would judge the wicked. She read through the entirety of them.

Next were Solomon's Proverbs. Many of them were about "forget not my law" and "these six things doth the Lord hate" — but she got only as far as 1:8 when she felt she had to stop:

My son, hear the instruction of thy father, and forsake not the law of thy mother; for they shall be an ornament of grace unto thy head, and chains about thy neck.

She closed her Bible then. What instruction had her father given? What law had her mother kept? She was the resulting accident of her mother's affair with a (married?) nobleman — the fruit of lawlessness, of betrayal to God's ways! How was she to resolve these questions, of her duty to parents and her obedience to God, who evidently also wished for her to act with duty to parents?

As Honoria occupied herself in the library, multiple young gentlemen were coming in hopes of calling upon her, but per instructions each was told that she was away. Cards were left that she might know they had attended upon her, and the boys left in turn.

By dinnertime, it was reasonable to expect no more visits would come, and so Honoria willingly came downstairs without fear of being seen. The Everdeens were uniformly perplexed by her behavior but she was offering no answers regarding her reasons.

She sat down to dinner, and having little to describe about her day, listened patiently to the tales of Margaret and Elizabeth and their exciting adventures in sock-buying that had gone forward without her. After the meal, as the family sat occupying themselves in the long evening light, Honoria had the opportunity to see whose cards had been left.

She had every expectation of seeing Lord Charles's name, as he had said that he would call; and indeed his card was included amongst the selection. However, to her fascination, the name of the Earl de Ryall was also upon one of the little slips of paper! She had not danced with him — whyever could he have been visiting?

She had not spoken to him since the evening when he had very kindly offered her a ride home — one that in retrospect she should have accepted — and afterwards paid a visit to the villainous next-door neighbor. She had many questions to ask of him, and she regretted immediately that she had refused to be "at home" to anybody, since she would have very much liked to have seen de Ryall.

$$\infty \cdot \infty$$

That night, Honoria bundled up in her dark room full of books, thinking of Lord de Ryall. She had not been able to spend a lot of time with him, nothing near what she would have liked. He had made the appearance of being a virtuous, kind, and perfectly mannered fellow. Was her guess about him incorrect? Had he been visiting the Viscount — such an unsavory character who took visits from women all night long? Was de Ryall a secret rake himself? Should she take Mr. Burney's advice and forget him? She began to fall asleep to these thoughts; and then, just at the moment when she ought to have drifted off into the shadows of slumber, an idea struck against her brain and woke her at once:

What if the Viscount was not a bad person, and thus it was perfectly decent for everyone to be visiting him?

Now, for women to be calling upon a man, unless he was a relative, for practically any reason was supposed to be unsavory no matter if he was a decent person or not. It was enough to ruin a woman's reputation. But then... might it be that the Viscount *was* receiving visits from numerous sisters, cousins, or other female relations? Could *that* be the reason they so readily came to call upon him at all hours?

And as she considered all of this, suddenly she realized something else: The Marquess, and Lord Charles, were her relations. It would be entirely decent if *she* came to call upon them.

The next morning, Honoria announced to the Everdeens her intention to pay a visit to the Marquess of Clarendon. Mr. Burney had advised

her not to reveal the identity of her father unless anyone needed to know, and it seemed that this was a situation where they needed to know. The Everdeens were amazed.

"You mean to simply call upon him, unannounced?" asked Edward in astonishment.

"I have attempted to gain introductions by other means, and have not been successful. It is a happy chance that he should be in Bath at the same time as I, and I have only a few weeks left of this visit. I should not like to miss this opportunity. It could never come again." Such was Honoria's response.

It seemed on the one hand an unwise choice, like Honoria might risk offending the Marquess; but on the other hand, her reasons were sound. If other means of introduction had not worked, what else could she do?

"You will be discreet about it?" asked Elizabeth with concern. "Certainly you will not go barging in, or declaring to everyone that you are his relation... consider that if even *you* did not know until recently, of how you were related, there might be others who have been rightly kept out of this secret."

"I intend to keep it as secret as I reasonably am able, but there are some who should have to know it, lest they think I am merely some female calling upon him," said Honoria.

"But consider," pleaded Edward, "that he might not *wish* for this to be known. Certainly it cannot be your desire to offend your father, or to bring him shame? For you to wish to meet him is not an unworthy intention by itself, but if it requires bringing him discomfort or humiliation, perhaps even stirring up ire in others who had not known of his past, how worthy is it, then?"

Honoria was forced to admit Edward's point. The Marquess alone, and none other, should know of her relation... but then, what would everyone else think of her calling at the house? She would be taken for some harlot! Yet when she complained of this predicament, the Everdeens were unable to help.

"Those seem to be your only options," said Elizabeth. "Either risk the loss of your reputation, or divulge your father's secret."

An hour later, Honoria was inside a sedan chair, *en route* to the house of the Marquess of Clarendon. Lord Charles's calling card was in her hand, and might be used as the cover for her visit. Yes, she was ready to do it — she was going to put her reputation on the line.

Sedan chairs were typical transport in the city of Bath, and had the advantage that it allowed her to travel alone; Elizabeth would have insisted upon attending with her, otherwise, and that would have been a negative for multiple reasons. She was happy that the chairmen seemed to know the location she had requested only by the name "Lord Clarendon's place," as the fact was that she had no idea where Lord Charles or the Marquess were living. As she was borne to the destination, it occurred to her that Lord Charles had said the Marquess was married. Perhaps anyone who saw her visiting might assume that she was there to call upon the Marchioness? The thought brought her a little bit of comfort and encouragement.

She was taken to the Crescent. How, she wondered, could she not have guessed that they would live in the Crescent — the most fashionable spot in all of Bath? She paid the exhausted chairmen who had carried her up such a steep hill, and then knocked at the first door she saw.

A porter answered the door. Honoria nervously asked if she might see the Marquess. The servant replied by telling her she was at the wrong house, and that she wanted the next one over. Humiliated already, Honoria thanked the servant as graciously as her shame would allow, and she went to the building indicated.

Already feeling that there was no hope that she would survive this with her dignity intact, she knocked again. Another servant, this one in green livery, came and, when she asked if she could see the Marquess, he attempted to turn her away as it was clear that she had no appointment and did not know him. Honoria nearly had to put her foot in the door in order to be able to present the card from Lord Charles.

"His son had promised an introduction," she said, holding the piece of paper with the name *Charles Montblank* upon it in calligraphy.

The servant took the card, and was apparently moved by its power. He showed her in, apologizing for having almost turned her away. "I ask you wait here, and I shall see if Lord Clarendon or his son are able to receive you at this time. What is your name again?"

"Honoria Wright — *daughter of Deborah Wright.*"

The servant did not make any indication of finding the name to be remarkable. He scurried up the stairs.

The wait seemed like an eternity. Honoria was full of questions. What if this was the wrong Marquess? What if he was not at home — or pretended he was not at home?

The worries were made moot when she was called up to see him; and this brought no relief to her, instead only intensifying her dread and hesitation. Her young face was suddenly beaded with perspiration. A horrible fear shook her, a trembling crept under her skin; and then suddenly a calm ensued, the suffering ceased, and her curiosity was lost. Perhaps, she thought, she did not really need to meet her father. She remained, stupefied, on the stairway; the footman needed to urge her along. Finally, she stiffened against the shame, mounted the dim stairway, and ran two steps at a time to the drawing room, despite the efforts of her hem to hold her back.

The Marquess was waiting for her, and Lord Charles was at his side. The Marquess looked pale, and acted with an extreme dignity that yet betrayed irritation. Lord Charles seemed to be ignorant of the significance of what was happening.

"Miss Wright," he said, seeming very amused at her presence. "I understand that you had missed my call yesterday, and so, it should seem, you have made the exceedingly unusual decision to come and visit me."

Honoria was very hesitant to answer. She looked at the Marquess. Their eyes met, and she could recognize a few of her own facial features upon him — the angle of the eyebrows, the point of the chin.

"Yes," Honoria answered to Lord Charles. "You, and your father, to whom you had promised me an introduction." Since Lord Charles was always so forward with her, she did not see any point to being considerate towards him now.

Lord Charles gave the introduction casually, changing his tone slightly in deference to his father, but seemingly delighted at how this girl was debasing herself before him. The Marquess then announced:

"Charles, leave the two of us alone to speak."

Lord Charles was very surprised at this, and his expression transformed in an instant. His sense of amusement vanished. "Leave you alone...? Why, you do not already know one another, do you?"

Honoria left it to the Marquess to explain.

"She is a relative of ours," he replied to his son. "I have not seen her in a long while. Leave us, and allow us to converse. I shall call when we are finished."

And so the bewildered Lord Charles left the room, wondering if Honoria was some kind of cousin about whom he had not known.

What was said between Honoria and the Marquess was unknown to anyone else; but over an hour later, both smiling as if their meeting had been agreeable, footmen were called to show Honoria out. She went away without speaking again to Lord Charles.

Returning to the drawing room where his father sat, Lord Charles inquired about their meeting. The Marquess said nothing of it, but instead informed his son: "You are not to pursue that lady any further. She is a *member of your family*; that is all you need to know."

And though he had not said it, Lord Charles was able to guess at what was meant. He turned pale, realizing the many impure thoughts he had conjured about his half-sister.

CHAPTER 10

Honoria hired a chair to take her back to the Everdeen house at Broad Street. She felt elated. Though she had no reason to think that the Marquess was going to publicly acknowledge her or anything of that sort, she was glad to have finally met, and learned something about her father. She had wondered what kind of man he was, what should have allowed him to enact the things he had — to impregnate some unmarried girl and leave her, abandoned. What she learned was that really, he had no tale of great love behind it, no tragic romance, no innocent explanations for how he always meant to make it right; but at the same time, he was no cackling villain, no wanton ruiner of virgins, no devil in disguise. It confused her, in a way; but she was happy to know it. Her mother too, according to him, had been a nice, decent girl, but she had gone along with his bad influence and next they knew, Honoria was born.

It was a troubling thought to Honoria that a decent girl could be moved to ruin herself by something so trivial. It made her think less of her mother somehow — she had always vaguely imagined, before, that her mother had been in some great romance, or at least moved by promises of marriage. But it seemed that her parents were far more ordinary than that. Common. Sinful.

Upon her return home, she greeted the Everdeens happily, and told them little of her encounter beyond that she had indeed met her father, and that their visit had been a pleasant one. The Everdeens were glad for her, and withheld themselves from any questions — such talk they already had posed to one another in her absence, and they were contented enough with their speculations that they did not need to know the truth.

Later in that afternoon, close to the end of acceptable visiting hours, another visitor for Honoria came to the house. It was Lord de Ryall.

Elizabeth and Margaret sat with her as she received him.

"I am so sorry," he began, "for having so continually come whilst you were away."

"Oh, you must not think I have reason to be displeased," said Honoria, "you only came yesterday."

"As a matter of fact, I have come several times."

"Really? Elizabeth, did we have any cards from him?" asked Honoria turning to her cousin; Elizabeth seemed perplexed, as if she knew of none.

"I did not leave any," said Lord de Ryall, "I feared you might view it as an imposition."

Now Honoria was bewildered at the levels of his good manners. "Why should that be any imposition?"

"I would not wish you to feel that I was calling upon you too often, or that you should be obligated to return a visit."

Honoria's amazement led her to pause before she realized that she ought to speak again. "Where are my manners? Please, Lord de Ryall, take a seat."

De Ryall took an armchair near Honoria, but not so near Honoria as it could seem indecent.

"I actually am very glad that you called," said Honoria, "for when I observed that you had given your card, I became most anxious to see you."

"Oh, dear! I am so sorry. That is very much what I was afraid of," said de Ryall. "I honestly did not wish to upset you!"

They then sat down and talked pleasantly of pleasant subjects. Lord de Ryall was perfectly amiable, and perfectly well-mannered. Honoria did her best to keep up with him.

What would Lord de Ryall think if he knew about her background?

What would he say if she asked him about that night at the vauxhall, and his presence at the house after the fact?

If she overtly asked him what he thought of her, what would he say?

That was a topic of much secret concern to Honoria. So often she observed that Lord de Ryall was about, but not talking to her. Was it out of politeness? Or was it out of contempt, or a desire to distance himself from her? These were all questions she longed to ask, yet could not bring herself to do in front of Margaret and Elizabeth. They needed some privacy, or something near enough to it.

And then, just before Lord de Ryall left, Honoria made a very pointed mention of the fact that she intended to go to the Pump Room on the following morning. "I think I shall be there about noontime," she said.

Lord de Ryall seemed to understand, and before he left, he promised that he would look for her there.

❧ · ❧

As ever, the poor and infirm were settled off to one corner, waiting to take their reviving waters from the pumps which gave the Pump Room its name. The rest of the space was filled with the fashionable, parading around or gathered in little cliques. Men in their breeches and white stockings, women in gold-embroidered gowns, circled the room as the musicians played in their nook above them.

Honoria entered, wearing her best dress. By now she was fairly adept at walking in it, with only a rare catch of her ankles threatening to trip her. Elizabeth was behind her as chaperone, dressed not to distract.

Honoria had arrived right on the money at noon, having cut her own breakfast short to be certain of making the appointment. She circled the room once with Elizabeth, searching faces, heart sinking as she was seeing nobody she recognized.

Then when she circled the second time, she observed him: Lord de Ryall, handsomely dressed in *demi-habillé*, entering with an anxious but hopeful look upon his face. He scanned the crowd for a moment before his gaze fell upon the fair Honoria. He hurried for her as fast as the throngs would permit him. Honoria stood waiting for him, her happy excitement forcing a bright flush of her cheeks.

De Ryall moved through the crowd without taking his gaze from the eyes of Honoria. Soon, they stood face to face, hardly space enough for air to separate them. This was the first time they had stood so near that she was able to realize just how tall he truly was. Honoria's eyes were right at the level of de Ryall's neckerchief. Ruffles stood out from his waistcoat.

The band played a tune in D minor, as de Ryall politely offered his hand and asked, "Shall we go round for the promenade?"

Joyously, Honoria took him by the ungloved hand, and they promenaded over and over, until they were breathless and flushed.

They hastened together to refresh themselves at the pump, while Elizabeth kept a polite distance behind them so that they might talk; Honoria only had a few weeks left in Bath, and she wanted to encourage whatever progress she might.

As the young pair sipped from cups of hot spa water, Honoria chose to ask of Lord de Ryall a most nagging question.

"Lord de Ryall, I must know — are you in fact acquainted with our neighbor at the Everdeen house? I believe the man is a Viscount?"

"You mean Lord Winthrope?" asked de Ryall, not thinking it very significant. "Of course. You saw how he helped me, when I was awaiting your safe return from the carriage-ride with Lord Charles. He offered me a decent excuse to stay out and wait for you."

"So he helped you?" asked Honoria, not focusing on the element which de Ryall had hoped she would note. "So then he is a good man?"

"Tolerably so," answered de Ryall. "He never looks to harm anyone, loves poetry, and I believe he even wrote an opera. Have you not met him?"

"I have not had the pleasure," said Honoria, feeling much relieved. "But I am glad to hear he is of good character. I had been concerned, seeing so many women going into his house; but I take it that they are sisters, or cousins to him?"

De Ryall looked a bit embarrassed. "Sisters...? I suppose that he does have *one*," he replied.

Now Honoria was flustered. What was going on then? "You mean to say the ladies who visit him are not relatives?"

"Not to him," replied de Ryall.

"But you said that he is a good man!" gasped Honoria. She was once again appalled.

"He is not a *bad* man," assured de Ryall. "Yes, he does receive women — normally, married women — at his house in a way that is contrary to custom. He takes whatever blows to his honor that creates for him, but he does it. That he *has* honor to damage, I think is a point in no dispute."

"And you associate yourself with such a man?" asked Honoria, wide-eyed in dread of what he would reply.

De Ryall could see the hurt in her eyes at his lack of perfection. He puffed his chest forward, ready to take whatever retaliation she was ready to dispense, over what he needed next to say. "My dear Honoria. I do not condone his activities, but to disdain a fine and intelligent man for them, is advantageous only to a person who is too much a dunderhead to be capable of observing an activity without imitating it. Am I such an ape? None but saints are perfect.

Mankind is full of flaws. Who are we to judge? The same man you look upon with disdain for the women he receives, disdains me because of the flaws he perceives me to possess; he thinks that my Jamaican investments are more immoral than his infringements upon marital rights and his visits with women of easy virtue. But we remain friends; we must hate the sin only, whilst loving the sinner. It is as one can observe with you and Lord Charles, who, despite his unbecoming behavior, you show such preference..."

"Preference!" gasped Honoria. "Oh, no, sir! You have it all wrong! I show him only politeness, and familial duty."

"Familial duty!" said Lord de Ryall, now himself perplexed. "Is he — a cousin?"

"He is my brother by half," answered Honoria before realizing what she had said. At once she regretted it. Quickly she added, "Please, do not advertise that fact to anyone."

Lord de Ryall responded with a smile of the utmost relief. "My dear Honoria, I was wrong — there is nobody in this world perfect but saints, *and you*."

Honoria smiled at his words, but without comprehending the reason behind them. The truth was that de Ryall had *assumed* Honoria's late-night carriage ride with Lord Charles had led to some sort of coition; for he knew Lord Charles too well not to guess at his motivations. He himself had been willing to forgive it. Lord de Ryall was like that. But now he was elated to learn there was no overlooking or forgiveness necessary. Honoria was the very embodiment of perfection!

As the pair began to return to the floor for more promenading, Honoria caught her foot on the hem of her skirt again, and sank. She dreaded that she would fall flat upon her face; but Lord de Ryall caught her, and her stumble was hardly even to be noticed. She was embarrassed and looked at him to thank him.

De Ryall smiled back at her. "I saw nothing," he said, thus assuring her that he did not hold the stumble as any marr upon her.

And the pair returned happily to the promenade.

A few more balls were danced, a few dinners were had. Then, on the day that Honoria Wright was due to depart from the city of Bath to return to her hometown of Blore, Lord de Ryall came to the house, and requested to speak with her alone.

To speak alone was only ever asked when a man had a marriage proposal in mind; and thus the Earl de Ryall made his plea to Honoria: he offered her his fortune, title, and his heart. Honoria accepted all of them graciously and with the utmost amiability.

It was now felt to be all the more of an honor for the Everdeens to have Honoria with them. She was the future Countess de Ryall! Although Honoria was beginning to feel homesick for Mr. Burney, it was decided that she was better off remaining in Bath until after her wedding, as there was no point returning to the tiny village of Blore only to have to leave again in a few weeks for the ceremony.

After receiving the news of what had happened, Mr. Burney sent his foster-daughter all his most heartfelt congratulations, and also sent to her some money which he informed her should be spent on a trousseau, the makings of which she was in a better position to choose than was he.

At the dressmaker's, Honoria ordered for herself several gowns based on the French fashions, including a special one of white silk with gold embroidery, that was now to be her wedding dress. It probably cost more than every other dress she had ever owned put together. Still, she was pleased that the long train of the gown opened up the skirt a bit, making it unlikely that she should trip from its narrowness.

Reverend Burney arrived at the Everdeen's a few days before the wedding, and to make room for him at the Everdeen's the servant's quarters were turned over to him, while the poor chambermaids were made to sleep on the kitchen floor.

In those days weddings were not normally grand affairs; but the wedding of an Earl attracted much attention, and the aristocrats wanted to observe the new person entering their ranks. It seemed surprising to some that Earl de Ryall was to marry a nobody: and to those who believed Honoria to be a drunk or a sponge, it was surprising that she was to marry so well.

Then, the day before the ceremony, the Bath newspapers contained an article mentioning that the marriage of the Earl de Ryall was expected to take place to Honoria Wright, the natural daughter of the Marquess of Clarendon.

It was Edward who first saw the article, and brought it to the attention of Honoria and Mr. Burney. They were both shocked and appalled at the announcement. Mr. Burney worried over how anyone had been able to figure out the identity of Honoria's father. Meanwhile, Honoria worried — how was the Marquess to react upon seeing such news in print?

The next morning, at Bath Abbey, an unusually large crowd for a wedding was gathered. It was mostly would-be socialites and curious members of the nobility, coming to gaze upon the new couple, and the new wedding fashion. Honoria, when she arrived with her party in a borrowed coach, was very surprised to see them all. There were a few faces she recalled from her parties at the Lauristons and Vauxhall. And then, as she scanned the crowd, she was surprised to see among the familiar faces that of the Marquess of Clarendon himself! She was at once both pleased and ashamed by his presence, for she was certain he must have heard about the ceremony by way of the newspaper.

Lord de Ryall awaited in a pale colored suit, and the ceremony proceeded in the usual manner. Rings were exchanged, and at the conclusion, the bells of the abbey were rung in their honor. When the ceremony was finished, and various attendees came to wish the couple well, the Marquess was among them.

Upon seeing him, the very first words out of Honoria's mouth were terms of apology, for she was very embarrassed that the word had somehow been leaked about their relationship.

The Marquess was not displeased at all. "Do not fret yourself, Lady de Ryall. It was I who publicly acknowledged the relationship, some weeks ago."

Honoria was amazed — that he would choose to reveal such a shameful thing, at long last! "Why should you have done so?" she asked.

"There was little reason to hide you anymore. You have done a father proud. May your marriage be a long and happy one," he said with a smile.

There was nothing more Honoria could say to that. From there, the new-made Earl and Countess proceeded with their invited guests, to the wedding breakfast.

END.